Mentor
An *Impossible* Novella

By Julia Sykes

Julia Sykes
© 2014

Author's Note

Before you read *Mentor,* I feel the need to explicitly
and emphatically warn you that this book deals with
dark themes that many readers will find disturbing.
This is not a romance. There is no Hero in this
story. There is no antagonist, either. This is the
story of two people trying to find sanity – and
possibly redemption – in a horrific situation.

I would warn you not to purchase this book if you
are worried it will upset you, but I won't bother
with that. This book *will* upset you. But if I've
managed to get it right, it will also intrigue you, and
possibly even tug at your heartstrings.

In September 2013, the FBI became aware of the existence of a sadistic psychopath who is abducting women. His identity is still unknown; he goes by the alias "The Mentor." This is the story of his relationship with the first woman he ever abducted.

Prologue

The Mentor

April 20, 1978

I slinked further into the shadows, concealing myself in the darker shades of night. The tremor in my hands came not from apprehension or hesitancy, but from anticipation.

I waited for my victim.

Soon, the darkness within me would be released, the pressure siphoned off. She would take my darkness. I would impart it to her, inflict it upon her.

I would be able to breathe again.

Seeking to still my shaking, I immersed myself in the memory of the first and only time the enigmatic pressure within me had been released.

Screams. Blood. Death.

Power. Freedom. Absolution.

I realized now that I hadn't really been alive before the day the light left my father's eyes. His lifeblood spilled over my hands, and the dulling film of perpetual apathy that coated my psyche dissipated. The world became sharp, my senses impossibly heightened. It was the closest thing to human emotion I had ever experienced. The pleasure that flooded me was the nearest approximation I could imagine to what normal people called joy.

But now the memory of that hyper-awareness – that sensation of being *alive* – tormented me as much as it pleased me.

No sooner had I disposed of my father's body than the sensation began to fade, and the dim monotony of my detached existence began to seep back into me. Now that I was aware of it, the dimness built, gathering slowly into darkness. My darkness.

It coiled within me, slithering through my veins and rendering my very pulse sluggish. It would overcome me, would consume me from the inside out, if it didn't find release.

Killing again wasn't an option. I might not have a formal education, but I wasn't stupid. I wasn't going to leave a trail of bodies behind and risk being caught.

If I kept *her* with me, she could take my darkness regularly. I would allow it to consume her rather than me. I would train her to like it. Otherwise, my darkness would devour her completely, and I would have to find a new toy. I couldn't risk drawing attention to myself by taking more than one woman.

Kathleen Marie White wasn't special to me in any way. No one was special to me. I had chosen her because she was convenient and she suited my needs.

Like me, she practically lived at the Hesburgh Libraries at the University of Notre

Dame. She had come here to study for the last four years, and even though I was a few years younger than she, I had been coming here for much longer than that.

I wasn't a student, but I had always found solace at the library. The desire to avoid my father and my disinterest in mundane human interactions made it an ideal place for me to hide out. People couldn't speak in the library. The pointless tedium of social pretentiousness was muffled within those walls.

As always, she was the last to leave the library on a Saturday night. The light of the streetlamp near the entrance caught the reddish facets of her dark hair, crowning her head with a crimson halo for the space of a moment.

My mind conjured up images of how I might draw that blood red shade from her body in other ways. Something unfamiliar stirred low in my gut in response, and my pulse jumped past its normal tempo.

Interesting.

I had intended to use sexual torment against her. Sex held little appeal for me; it would simply be a means to an end. But in that moment, I understood its allure. When used as a weapon, sex might be pleasurable. The sudden stiffening of my cock told me as much.

I clenched my fingers into hard fists, willing their increased trembling to stop.

Control.

Control yourself. Control the darkness.

Soon, I would control *her*, and the darkness would never rule me again. I would be alive. More than that, I would revel in the heady power I had experienced as my father's life slipped away under my hands. She would give that to me daily.

She turned from locking the library doors, and I caught sight of her face. It was lovelier than I had realized. She wasn't perfect by conventional standards, but the hint of a contented smile that played around the corners of her mouth gave off a sense of innocence that was undeniably appealing. Her deep green eyes were large, only further lending to that vision of purity.

When I had watched her over the last four years, her beauty had been obscured by unconscious nervous habits. Usually, a small furrow persisted between her brows as she bent over a book, and her full lips were thinned while she chewed at a pencil.

I had chosen her for that very reason. Drive and determination were evident in every line of her body as she studied furiously every day. She thought she could shape her own destiny if she just worked hard enough.

But her fate was no longer hers to govern. What she surely considered her greatest assets – her tenacity and intellect – were the very qualities which would lead to her ruination at my hands.

There would have been no satisfaction in breaking a weak woman. Kathleen Marie White was exactly what I needed.

No, it was more than that. More than need. *Want.*

I wanted something. The realization was jarring, the sensation utterly new. My lips curled upward in a semblance of a smile, and my hand was rock steady as I reached into my pocket to retrieve the ether-soaked rag.

I would take what I wanted.

Chapter 1

Kathleen

Are you going to kill me?

The sharp tang of instinctive fear was a taste at the back of my throat. Or maybe that was the acrid burn of the bile that rose as my head spun and my stomach churned.

The world was black. I tried to open my eyes, but something pressed tightly against them, holding my lids closed. I sucked in a gasp and immediately gagged when cloth shifted to touch the inside of my throat. My tongue sought to push out the invasive object, but the knot remained firmly drawn between my teeth. I reached up to rip it from my mouth. I was stopped short, something rough biting into my wrists. My arms jerked ineffectually.

The cloth between my lips absorbed my scream before my mind fully processed my situation. Thoughts were unable to coalesce in the wake of the torrent of terror that surged through my system.

Restrained. Blindfolded. Gagged.
Wake up! Wake up!

This wasn't the first time I had been trapped in an all-too-vivid nightmare. Ever since I was a child, I had been plagued by dreams of being trapped, powerless, and afraid. Dreams fueled by memories are cruelly potent.

But none had ever been as visceral as this one.

My body fought, thrashing. Bruises bloomed beneath the surface of my skin as I twisted against the ropes that bound me securely to the unyielding metal chair.

Dread pulsed to life, mingling with the panic that thrummed through my veins to create a horrific cocktail. Even in nightmares, pain was an ephemeral, intangible thing. My dreaming mind told me there was pain, but my body knew that my nerve endings weren't actually screaming from damage. My mind honed in on the fact that my wrists and ankles were being rubbed raw.

Real. This is real.

A despairing sob punctuated the screams that continued to rip their way up my throat. The gag caught each of them, smothering the piercing cries to something faint and piteous.

Screaming would do me no good. It hadn't in the past, and it wouldn't help me now.

Breathe. Think.

It had taken me years to overcome this primal fear. I had escaped its grip before; I could do it again. Taking several deep breaths, I calmed the convulsions that seized my chest with each wracking sob.

"Are you finished already?"

The softly spoken, broadly accented words were uttered just by my ear, jolting a fresh scream from deep within me. Warm breath played across my neck as the man laughed quietly. I twisted my head, instinctively seeking to identify the threat. The thick material pressed against my eyes kept my lids securely shuttered, rendering me blind.

"I was hoping for a longer show this first time. But that's all right. I'll sample each of your screams soon enough. No one can hear you down here." His whisper was a snake slithering across dry leaves, dread and dead things.

Dozens of questions should have been running through my mind. *Who are you? Where am I? Why are you doing this?* But everything was overridden by the terror that overtook me once again at the sound of his voice. There was no menace in it, only cold amusement and a thread of eager anticipation.

Run run run run run!

My heart beat wildly against my ribcage, seeking the escape that my immobilized body was unable to attain.

I heard him inhale deeply, felt him suck the air away just by my cheek. His nose grazed along my jawline, sampling my fear in the same way a lover might revel in his partner's arousal. I shuddered at the feather-light, intimate contact. It was as though he had stolen all of the oxygen in his one indulgent breath, and my lungs seized, choking off my cries.

"If you're done screaming, I'm sure you have questions. I promise to answer all of them honestly. But know that each one will cost you something. If you want to be treated like a human being, you have to earn it. From now on, your humanity is a privilege, not a right. Your body is my plaything, your pain my favorite toy."

Rape. Torture.

The sickening words thrummed to life deep in my mind, but my conscious thoughts were too busy, too frightened, to face them.

Before I could, the knotted cloth pressed further into my mouth, and I gagged as it brushed the back of my throat again. Then it loosened, and I shoved it free with my tongue. I gulped in cool air. It burned down my raw throat.

"Please." It was a strangled, unintelligible croak. I swallowed hard, willing my tightened throat to relax enough to allow words to pass through it. "Please," I managed to rasp. "Let me go. Please don't hurt me."

Something cold and razor-thin traced a chill line down the column of my throat. I stopped speaking, stopped breathing for fear that one small movement would cause the knife to slice through my delicate skin.

"You belong to me now. You're not going anywhere."

"Are you going to kill me?" The question that was imperative to my next breath came out in a rush.

He sighed, a long, happy exhalation. I could practically feel the perverse pleasure pulsing off him.

The blade slid down past my collarbone, but it didn't so much as prick my skin. Instead, it settled behind the top button of my blouse. There was a slight tug, followed by a popping sound as the tiny false pearl bounced across the hard ground. Before my mind could fully process the horror, another button hit the floor, and a chill raced across my skin where my shirt fell open, exposing me.

No one had ever looked upon even this small amount of my bare flesh. I had never wanted anyone to see that much of me. Disgust rolled through me as the monster bared me to a man's eyes for the first time.

I twisted uselessly against my bonds. "Please, stop! Don't do this!" The words were stilted, stupid, useless.

"You did this to yourself," he told me. His voice was dispassionate, seemingly unaffected by my nudity despite his steady progress in stripping me. "You asked a question, and this is the price for your answer."

He allowed me to sob and beg, wielding the knife with exact, almost loving, precision. It never once pierced my flesh, not even when he hooked it beneath the waistband of my slacks and the side of my underwear, cleanly shearing through both in one smooth motion.

Only when I was completely naked, when I had paid the price, did he speak to me again.

"To answer your question: No. I'm not going to kill you. I'm going to keep you."

His fingertips brushed my bare waist, trailing slowly upward in a mockery of a caress. Pure revulsion rolled through me in a wracking shudder. My skin pebbled, and all of my fine hairs stood on end.

I tried in vain to jerk away from him. "Don't touch me!" My protest was the hiss of a cornered animal.

He ignored me, his fingers continuing their steady progress. They reached the outer curve of my breast, and his touch stuttered, turning almost tentative. I would have described his exploration as tender were it not for the fact that the shivers racing across my skin were a product of disgust rather than desire.

"I will touch you whenever I want, pet. One day, you'll come to crave it. You'll beg me for the feel of my hands upon you."

As though to make up for his moment of hesitation, he gripped my breast hard, his fingers digging into the tender flesh. The flare of pain was shocking in the wake of his gentle touches.

"You'll come to crave the pain as well," he promised in a low murmur.

"You're insane!" The accusation came out on something between a defiant scream and a fearful sob.

"You don't know the half of it. But you will."

His cruel grip eased, and his fingers massaged away the pain. My peaked nipple grazed against his calloused palm. Between my blindness and immobility, I was powerless to prevent all my focus from honing in on the sensation of his skin against mine. My nerve endings crackled, making me hyper-aware of my body in a way that was utterly foreign to me. No one had ever touched me like this; no one had ever touched me at all. Especially not these secret places.

He tweaked my hardened nipple, and his quiet laugh mingled with my shocked gasp. The sensation was… strange. I squirmed, noticing how warm my skin was against the cool metal chair.

"We're going to get along very well, pet," he assured me. It was the first time I had detected genuine warmth in his voice; it was a perverse, lustful heat. I noticed that his accent was a long drawl, lengthening his words and softening them in a way that belied their cruelty.

"Don't call me that!" My indignant snap was ruined by a fearful tremor. "My name is Kathleen. Kathleen Marie White. Please let me go. I have a life. I have a family," I lied. I would say anything to sway him.

"No. You don't." His fingers closed around my nipple again, pinching and twisting this time. My wild attempt to wrench away only doubled my pain. "I won't tolerate lies. I know who you are, Kathy."

"Kathleen. It's Kathleen." The correction was automatic, reinforced by years of practice. Kathy was what my father had called me.

His fingernails bit into me. I couldn't hold in my scream.

"I get to decide what to call my property, *pet*."

I started crying again, and my head shook back and forth. My mind denied what was happening to me.

He drew away from me, and I made a strange whimper as cool air rushed to fill the space where his heat had painted my skin. His footsteps echoed through my darkness.

"Where are you going?" My voice was high and thin with my sudden panic. His intimate touches had disgusted me, and his coldly amused words had terrified me, but fear of the unknown surged through me. I realized a second too late that I had asked a question. Automatically, I recoiled. My clothing had been forfeit for my first answer. What would he take this time?

"Wherever I feel like going." His tone was casual, but his meaning was clear. He was free; he had all the power. He was going to leave me here, trapped in the dark and caught under the sapping weight of my fear.

His footsteps retreated further, and I shrieked out my fury and terror.

"Let me go, you sick bastard! Let me go!" I jerked at my bonds, my body struggling for freedom. All I earned for myself was fresh pain as rope dug into my bare skin.

A door creaked open and thumped closed. A lock clicked into place. I screamed into the darkness.

His Journal

April 21, 1978

I can still hear her screaming. The sound just does something for me. In all my life, I've never felt this kind of desire. I've read about the lust that claims men from the time they hit adolescence, but it's never happened to me. I had thought that things like happiness and joy had been beaten out of me, rendering me incapable of pleasure. That never really bothered me before, not until I got my first taste of pleasure while I watched my father die in agony.

What she makes me feel is different. My father's end was too quick, driven by vengeance and the need to defend myself. Killing him made me feel powerful, but the heady sensation was fleeting.

If I keep her, I can control her. I can elicit her fear in bliss-inducing surges. For the first time in my life, I hold all the power.

She's so fragile. I could break her with my bare hands. I've never seen anything so beautiful.

My plan to allow her to question me turned out to be a stroke of brilliance. She's intelligent, that much has been obvious since I first saw her in the library. Her desire for knowledge will slowly force her to surrender everything to me. She will cede herself to me through the illusion of free choice that I allow her. I wonder how long it will take her to realize that her one perceived freedom is my most effective weapon in breaking her.

She's going quiet now. But even though her screams are dwindling, my arousal isn't. I had intended to use sexual touches to frighten her, but I might harvest pleasure from her in ways I had never imagined. I crave to use her body to slake this newfound need. It will take all of my willpower to wait. I need to learn her body, to understand how to best draw lust from her.

I promised her that she will crave my touch one day. I also promised that I

will be completely honest with her.
She will learn that, for all my
depravities, I am a man of my word.

Chapter 2

Kathleen

Who are you?

I entered a strange delirium, a state where exhaustion warred with my fear to keep me in some horrible state where I couldn't differentiate between sleep and wakefulness. In my blindness, the lucid dreams of my painful past and the horrors of my present intermingled.

"What the fuck is this, Rachel?" My father bellowed, his words slurred with his drunkenness.

"Roger." His name was a fearful gasp on my mother's lips. "I'm sorry. It's all we could afford."

Daddy angrily swiped the meager meal away. The porcelain plate shattered against the wall. Even at the age of seven, I knew that he had drunk away the money that should have bought us a proper meal.

Mommy did nothing but apologize, but Daddy's face turned a dangerous shade of purple that I recognized all too well.

My sister and I ducked beneath the table just before the resounding smack *of Daddy's hand against Mommy's face cracked through the small kitchen. Bea cringed against me and gripped my hand with her small fingers. She was only five, but she understood violence and pain as well as I did.*

Mommy, run! Why doesn't she run? *I didn't know why she didn't try to escape him when he hurt her so terribly. That was something I would learn later, but I would never understand it.*

Passion is a double-edged sword, and I wanted no part of it.

The echoes of my father's enraged screams pounded against the inside of my skull, the pain a reminder of abuse. But the harsh sting of abrasions around my wrists and ankles was new.

I almost longed to remain immersed in my dark memories. At least they were securely in my past; the horrors of my present were too terrible to contemplate.

My discomforts cruelly pulled me firmly back into my new reality. My shoulders screamed in protest at their prolonged imprisonment, and the unyielding metal slats of the chair to which I was bound dug into my back. I tried to swallow to alleviate some of the rawness in my throat, but my tongue was sandpaper.

How long had I been here? How long since I had tasted food or water? My stomach felt hollow, and even my veins seemed parched and withering.

Surely my captor wouldn't leave me here to die. He had said he wanted to *keep* me.

The idea made my empty stomach churn, even as I longed for him to return and grant me reprieve from my thirst and hunger.

Trapped in the dark and engulfed by pain, I had no concept of the passage of time. I only knew that by the time the door creaked open, I was desperate for him. My small moan at the sound was wrought of relief rather than fear.

"I think you've suffered long enough, pet." The softness of his words might have been mistaken for caring, but I knew better. *He* was the one who had inflicted my suffering, so his decision to end it wasn't a show of concern.

My discomfort was the price for my question, and he had finally deemed that the price was paid.

"Where are you going?"
"Wherever I feel like going."

What use was that? He had promised that each question would have an honest answer, and each answer would have a cost. I had cost myself dearly with my rash query. I would have to be more careful with my words if I was going to get out of this place with my sanity intact.

I resolved not to ask any more questions. I couldn't afford to lose anything else to him.

There was a strange sloshing noise before me.

Water.

I pulled against my bonds, blindly searching for what I needed.

His fingertips caressed my cheek, and I jolted at the sudden contact. There was moisture on his skin, and it kissed my dry lips as he traced his thumb across them. I couldn't help myself; my tongue darted out to catch the droplets of water, caressing his flesh as I did so. He tasted slightly salty, but the water was sweet. It was the most delicious thing I could ever recall.

"You must be very thirsty." His voice was low and a bit husky, as though he was affected by the touch of my tongue.

More. I needed more. To my shame, I parted my lips, seeking to taste him again. His thumb pressed between them, and I yielded easily to the gentle pressure. My mouth closed around him, greedily sucking away every droplet of the precious liquid.

"That's it, pet. Good girl."

Revulsion suddenly gripped my gut.

What am I doing?

I bit down hard, a furious growl escaping me. But he was ready, and in my blindness I hadn't been able to see his fingers hovering over either side of my jaw, ready to clamp down. They dug into my cheeks, forcing my mouth open before my teeth so much as grazed his skin.

I would have railed at him for being a sadistic bastard, but I couldn't manage to force out more than a croak.

"Well, if you're not thirsty…" He trailed off on a chuckle, and his feet scraped across the floor as he moved away from me, taking the life-giving water with him.

"No!" An unintelligible, desperate cry made its way up my ravaged throat. *"Please."* My cracked lips formed the word, my vocal cords giving up on forming coherent sound.

Shame returned, but I forced it to the edges of my consciousness. Survival was more imperative than my pride, and I had never felt closer to death.

His warm breath returned to my ear, and cold water dripped into the hollow at my throat. I whimpered as it trailed uselessly between my breasts. My tongue thrust out of my mouth, silently begging for more.

"Are you going to behave?" He asked sternly.

Hating him, I nodded.

Loathing faded to bliss when a drop of water hit my waiting tongue. When I pulled it back into my mouth to swallow, his wet forefinger thrust in. He was harsh, invasive this time. Instinctively, I tried to jerk away as his touch neared my throat, but his other hand closed around the back of my skull, blocking my retreat.

He stilled, waiting. Now that his hand was at the back of my head, I knew that he wouldn't be able to prevent me from biting him. I also knew that if I did so, he would leave me again, denying me the water I so desperately needed.

"It's your choice," he told me calmly. He knew what I was thinking, had predicted my actions. How many steps ahead was he?

Cold swept through me as I recognized my captor's intelligence. I was relying on my own mind to save me, but his was obviously formidable.

And this round undeniably went to him.

If I had the strength, I might have laughed madly. Did I really think I had a chance to beat him, to win? We weren't even playing a game; he was playing, and I was his toy.

I slumped in my seat, recognizing my defeat. I forced my mind to shut down completely, to ignore the anger and grief and humiliation. There would be time to try to out-think him later. For now, he held my life in his hands, and I was too desperate for sustenance to deny him.

"Good girl," he praised me again as I accepted him. I shuddered.

Slowly, he pulled his finger through my lips, dragging it along my tongue. It fought to keep him in, craving the moisture he offered.

Once he had fully extricated himself from my mouth, I heard the sloshing sound again. Seconds later, a blessed pool of water was at my lips. The cool liquid dripped over the side of his cupped palm onto my waiting tongue. It slid through his fingers to drizzle onto my throat, my breasts, my stomach. Every inch of my body was greedy for it, desperate to soak up as much as possible.

He repeated the process, not stopping until my tongue no longer felt sundried and shriveled. He appreciated its return to velvety smoothness by stroking two fingers into my mouth, sliding them in and out. I didn't even realize that I followed the pumping motion, trying to keep him – no, the water that lingered on his skin – in my mouth.

His low rumble of approval seemed to vibrate through me, but despite my self-loathing, I couldn't stop myself from whining in protest when he finally removed his hand completely.

"Don't be greedy, pet," he chided. "You take what I give you."

Before I could muster up the anger to snarl at him, something fleshy and wet pressed against my lips. The sweet melon touched my tongue, and its delicious juice burst in my mouth when I bit into it.

"Good behavior is rewarded."

"Fuck you, you sick bastard!" The words never managed to form on my tongue; it was too concerned with consuming as much of the honeydew as possible.

He was no longer gripping the base of my skull to hold me in place. Instead, his hand caressed my neck. His fingers played through my hair, massaging my scalp. The simple comforting touch helped ease some of the tension that had gripped me during my hours of tight bondage. I fought the urge to drop my head back, to welcome the contact. I didn't entirely succeed.

When my stomach no longer felt achingly empty, his fingers touched beneath my chin, silently closing my waiting mouth to let me know that he was finished feeding me.

Disgust rattled insistently at the edges of my consciousness, but I resolutely forced it back. I couldn't face the humiliation of what he had done to me. My behavior was abhorrent, but I hadn't had a choice.

Had I?

I should have died before accepting that treatment, I berated myself.

But self-deprecation wouldn't do me any good now. What was done was done.

Put it behind you. Move past it.

I had learned to ignore the horrors of my past long ago. I wouldn't have survived otherwise. That was all I could focus on for the time being: survival. I couldn't escape if I was dead. I had lived through abuse before, and I could do it again. I wouldn't let this bastard beat me.

The cold edge of the knife against the crook of my arm was now a familiar sensation.

"Don't move," he warned. Again, his soft tone was a perversion of caring. The man holding a blade against my skin wasn't concerned with my well-being. He was concerned with maintaining his control over me.

The rope briefly bit into the abrasions around my wrists, and I hissed in pain just before my bonds fell away. My tormentor had sliced through them as easily as he had cut away my clothes.

I had all but forgotten that I was naked. When base imperatives like hunger and thirst weren't met, the denial of social norms like covering one's nudity seemed unimportant. Now that my need for sustenance had been slaked, my discomfort at the sensation of his hands on my bare skin returned full-force.

But that was nothing compared to the humiliation he was about to force me to endure.

Once he had freed my ankles, his hands closed around my waist, pulling me upright. My cramped muscles shrieked in protest, and my legs gave way beneath me. I collapsed against him, and he caught me easily. My hands strained to lash out at him, but my arms hung uselessly at my sides.

One arm braced around my waist, and his other hand stroked up and down my back.

"Shhh," he soothed me.

A childlike sob ripped its way up my throat as an overwhelming surge of emotion tore through me: anguish, fear, fury, humiliation, and a sick sense of longing. I craved comfort, and his twisted parody of care tricked my shattered mind into accepting his touch.

The lingering desire to hurt him only filled me with that much more distress at the knowledge that there was nothing I could do against him. I could feel the muscles of his chest and arms undulating around me as he continued to stroke me. Even if I possessed the strength to fight him, my limbs were still screaming from their prolonged immobility.

I was powerless, and that was exactly how he wanted me to feel.

That knowledge helped me gather my wits. My sobs quieted, giving way to my determination to defy him. He might have control of my body, but I would deny him control of my mind.

He recognized the return of my willpower. Again, he proved that he was several steps ahead of me when he scooped me up into his arms. I gave a little shocked squeal at the disorienting movement. My sight was still denied me, depriving me of any sense of balance.

When he swung me down, my naked thighs came to rest on something cold and hard. I started crying again when I realized what it was: a toilet.

"Fuck you," I flung at him before my sobs robbed me of the ability to speak.

He said nothing; he just allowed me to cry while he petted my hair. His other hand held the flat of the knife across my throat, a silent warning not to fight him. For a moment, I considered leaning into the blade, to end this perverted torment. The psychological torture was so much worse than the physical pain he had inflicted upon me.

Death at the edge of his knife was a siren's call. The blade had so cruelly stripped me of so many things: my clothing, my dignity. Why not let it take my life? At least it would be on my own terms.

To my chagrin, I discovered that I was a coward; I just couldn't do it.

I'm not sure how long it took, but he simply waited until my needs overcame my resistance.

"I hate you," I managed to hiss when he lifted me up once again.

"I know." I could feel him shrug, as though my hatred was of no consequence to him. His casual demeanor was belied by the hint of pleasure in his voice. He wanted me to hate him. Even my loathing was a weapon to be used against me, an indulgence he savored.

I shuddered in his arms, but I had no more tears to cry.

He laid me down on something soft. I couldn't hold in a small sigh of relief that he hadn't returned me to the cruel metal chair.

Before I could even consider pushing through the pain in my stiff limbs to fight him, his hands closed around my upper arms. His fingers worked my sore muscles, and I couldn't hold in my moan as the tightness eased. I went limp beneath him, losing the will to resist.

Later. I'll fight later. I'm too weak now, I'm blind, and he has a knife.

Yes, later was definitely better.

His hands progressed along my arms, drawing them up above my head to stretch my shoulders while he massaged away the pain.

Suddenly, his weight settled over my hips, and his forearm pinned down my left wrist while he firmly grasped the right one.

"What-"

I stopped my panicked question just in time. *"What are you doing?"*

Something soft encircled my wrist, pulling tight just before a metallic tinkling filled my ears. The quiet *snick* was familiar, and it took me three horrified heartbeats before I accepted the meaning of the sound.

Padlock.

I struggled in earnest, wildly twisting beneath him, but his weight restrained me as efficiently as the rope that had held me to the chair.

He quickly repeated the process on my left wrist. I jerked against the restraints as soon as he released my hands, but my efforts were met with a clanking sound, and I realized that my range of movement was restricted to no more than a few inches.

His fingers gently traced down my arms. I felt something harder than his hips pressing into my belly.

I might have been a virgin, but I wasn't completely naïve. My captor was aroused by my struggles.

The knowledge increased the frenzy of my instinctive efforts to escape him.

"Shhh," he soothed me again, his hands caressing the outer swell of my breasts.

My nipples pebbled automatically at the touch, and bile rose in the back of my throat.

Rape. He's going to rape me.

"Don't." I couldn't manage to force out more than the one word.

"I'm not going to rape you, pet," he reassured me, reading my thoughts again. "You'll ask me to fuck you one day."

"You sick bastard!" I found my voice. "You're crazy!"

His hand closed around my throat. He didn't squeeze; it was a silent warning. I went still instantly, my damn survival instinct kicking me into obedience.

"I already told you: you don't know the half of it. But I won't tolerate such rude language. Pets aren't supposed to speak. Your words are a privilege, and you should be careful how you use them unless you want to lose that privilege."

I swallowed hard, and my body began to tremble. Even if I had dared to hurl more insults at him, the fear that clogged my throat would have prevented me from doing so.

Maintaining his hold on my neck, he abruptly ripped the blindfold from my eyes. The flood of light seared them, and I screamed as I clamped my lids closed.

"Please-"

I stopped myself before I could beg him to return me to the darkness. Not only did the light hurt, but I was terrified to face my reality, to face *him.* Somehow, the blindness had made it less real. If I opened my eyes, the world would take shape around me, and the horror of my situation would become concrete.

Coward, I accused myself. How could I ever hope to escape if I couldn't take inventory of my prison? I needed to learn everything I could about where I was and who my tormentor was if I wanted to see the outside world again.

I blinked hard, forcing my eyes to focus. The room seemed painfully bright, even though my mind registered the fact that it was only dimly lit. The shadows on my captor's face told me that much.

He shifted where he hovered above me, tilting his face up slightly to force the shadows to dissipate. Recognition jolted through my gut, and I gasped.

The boy from the library. The beautiful boy I had covertly watched from beneath my lashes as I studied. My commitment to excellence wasn't the only reason I had practically lived in that place for the last four years.

His cheekbones were high and sharply defined, the lines of his face angular and definitively masculine, despite his youthfully smooth cheeks. He couldn't have been more than twenty years old. Far too young to kidnap and terrorize a woman.

His spun-gold hair was simply but carefully styled, as always. His golden eyes would have matched it perfectly, were it not for the streaks of reddish-brown that shot through his irises. I had never noticed that before; I had never been close enough. The red might have turned them an alluring amber, but instead they called to mind something evil.

A perversely pleased demon stared down at me, his full lips twisted in what might be considered a smile.

No demon should be so beautiful. Perhaps he was a fallen angel, one of Lucifer's followers condemned to suffer in Hell for all eternity. Only, the creature above me didn't seem to be suffering. He reveled in his condemnation.

"Who are you?" My words were barely audible.

His smile widened to a grin that was almost dazzling in its perfection.

Definitely a fallen angel.

I realized my folly a moment too late. I had asked a question.

"I am your Master."

My stomach roiled. "No." The sickened protest was automatic, an involuntary denial. How could the boy I had secretly coveted be the man who was torturing me so mercilessly? Surely he was too young and innocent to be capable of such evil.

He grasped my jaw, stopping the shaking of my head.

"Yes," he told me firmly. "And you will address me properly when I allow you to speak."

"No." My voice wavered with my disbelief and mounting horror. "Oh, god. No."

This was the price for my question. I couldn't do it. I couldn't. I had already given up so much, had already paid so dearly for my mistakes. Surely he had taken enough of my dignity.

The gleam in his eye let me know that he wasn't satisfied with my dignity; he wanted my humanity. "Pet" wasn't an endearment. He intended to break me and make me his creature.

"I gave you an order, pet. And you will obey me."

His fingers closed around my nipples, twisting hard. I found my tears again.

I writhed, yanking against my restraints in a useless attempt to escape the pain.

"I won't!" I scraped together what was left of my defiance. "Let me go, you sick fuck!"

His fingers tightened, and I screamed.

"You will," he informed me calmly. "And what did I tell you about foul language?"

He clucked his tongue at me and shifted his weight. He gripped my thighs, forcing them apart before straddling my knees, pinning me in position. I was spread for him, completely open. No one had ever looked at this secret part of my body, not even me.

His hand came down on my inner thigh. The sharp *smack* resounded through the small room just before the pain hit. I gasped at the intensity of it, the shock robbing me of the breath I needed to cry out.

My screams started soon enough.

It only took three blows for me to begin begging for him to stop.

"I'll stop when you accept your place. Good behavior is rewarded. Disobedience will result in punishment." Another agonizing blow. "Address me properly, and I'll stop."

"Master!" I shouted quickly, unable to fight the pain any longer. There would be time to hate myself later. All I could think about was making it stop.

The slap of his hand on my abused flesh cracked through the room again.

"Yes? Did you have something you wanted to say to me, pet?"

"Stop. Ma-Master." I stumbled over the word.

His fingers dug into my bruised skin.

"Try again," he reprimanded.

"Please, Master. Please stop."

He tenderly stroked my enflamed thighs in reward. "Good girl."

I turned my face into the crook of my shoulder, hiding my eyes in shame. He continued to pet me as I cried and shook.

I hated the soothing sensation even as I reveled in the fact that it had replaced the pain, putting an end to my agony.

His Journal

April 22, 1978

The sound of "Master" on her lips is even sweeter than her screams. And the feel of her mouth around my fingers, of her writhing beneath my cock, is helping me to understand the meaning of the word "erotic."

Her intelligence only further stokes my interest. Even when her eyes were hidden by the blindfold, I could see her mind working in the furrow in her brow and the lines around her mouth. She still thinks she can beat me somehow. Only minutes after she called me Master, the renewed tautness in her muscles let me know that she was coming back to herself. She was definitely plotting something.

But I've been plotting, too, for far longer than she has. I've planned this for weeks, and she has no idea what's in store for her.

Toying with her elicits a pleasure
I've never known, and her moments
of defeat are pure rapture. I can
hardly wait for her next question.

Chapter 3

Kathleen

Why are you doing this?

I cringed at my shameful memories. My soul felt rawer than my torn skin where the rope had burned into me. The chafing on my wrists stung every time I shifted my arms, a constant reminder of my restraints.

My tormentor had replaced the blindfold, but before he left I had a few minutes to study my surroundings for weak points, assessing escape routes.

He had laid me out on a bed, where he had bound me with leather cuffs that were locked around my wrists and attached to the headboard by short chains. The cuffs were softer than the rope, but the tight bondage caused just as much despair.

The room in which I was being held appropriately resembled a dank dungeon, although my mind recognized it as a basement. It was dimly lit by one spare bulb above the bed. The walls were concrete block, their dull grey matching the concrete floor. Stairs to the left of the bed led up to a door, the only visible exit from the basement. Another door stood open, revealing the bathroom where I had been humiliated.

I almost welcomed the darkness of the blindfold. It shut out the terrifying world in which I was trapped.

Once my vision was black once again, the monster had even tenderly covered my body with a blanket to ward of the chill.

His sweet actions contrasted cruelly with his torturous ones. He pushed me to a point of weakness, then offered me comfort. While my mind was shattered from pain and fear, I couldn't help but react to that comfort. That disgusted me almost as much as my failure to resist calling him Master.

It had been years since I had sobbed against someone like that. The last time had been when I was twelve, crying into my mother's shoulder. I stopped doing that when I realized how weak she was. How could I find strength in the arms of someone who couldn't – who wouldn't – protect me?

I hadn't allowed Charlie to hold me like that, either. I also hadn't allowed him to gaze upon my naked body, to touch my most secret places. Even though he had told me he wanted to marry me, I hadn't allowed it.

Before my abduction, it had only been two weeks since he had asked me the question I had feared. In my darkness, it was all too easy to fall into the vivid memory.

"Will you marry me, Kathleen?"

Charlie stared up at me from where he rested on one knee, his deep blue eyes soft and earnest. His intentions were pure, but the question sent fear and a hint of revulsion coursing through me. The rush of joy most women felt in such a moment was absent in me.

"Charlie," I began hesitantly. "We've talked about this..."

His hands closed around mine, a tender, almost beseeching gesture.

"I love you, Kathleen. And I think you love me, too, if you'll just admit it to yourself."

"I... I do care about you, Charlie. But-"

"Then marry me," he cut across me almost desperately, refusing to let me turn him down.

I shook my head. "You don't want me, Charlie. Not really. You want a wife and kids and a white picket fence. I want a career. I'm sorry I've held on to you for so long..."

I swallowed hard at the sight of his shining blue eyes. They contrasted beautifully with his dark hair. He was too good-looking for me. He was too good for me in so many ways.

"I'm not right for you," I insisted. I was remotely surprised to hear the words come out in a ragged whisper. Regret and longing rose up in me.

Do I love him?

No. I couldn't. Even if I did love Charlie, I didn't love him enough to give up the life I wanted for myself.

"You don't mean that, Kathleen. I know you're scared because of what happened with your parents, but it won't be like that between us. I promise." He stood and cupped my cheek in his hand. I leaned into his touch without a thought. "I would never hurt you. I'll take care of you."

That last part got my hackles up. I didn't want to be taken care of. I could take care of myself.

He leaned in to kiss me, but I pulled away. I was afraid of his kiss, afraid of the rush of heat it would elicit from deep in my belly.

That was how men controlled women. Lust could make us surrender ourselves, and I wasn't going to let desire rule my life.

I turned my tear-streaked face away from him.

"I'm sorry, Charlie. I can't."

I almost regretted rejecting him. If I had accepted his proposal, would I have been alone, vulnerable to capture, on the night I was taken?

I bit my lip, wrestling with my thoughts.

Would I trade this hellish imprisonment for a different form of captivity? I had loathed the idea of being in a man's thrall. I had too much I wanted to do with my life; I didn't want the duties of a wife and mother. I had seen how coupling with a man could cost a woman her freedom, and I wanted no part of it.

The memory that thought elicited wasn't as fresh as Charlie's failed proposal, but it was no less sharp. Those few horrific minutes were burned into my brain.

My mother was crying again, her sobs punctuated by the sound of my father's hand punishing her. I could hear his enraged shouts clearly through the cracked door to their bedroom.

"God damn it, Rachel!"

"I'm sorry, Roger. I'm so sorry."

But I knew that my mother had done nothing wrong. She never did, but he hit her anyway. She took the hits for Bea and me, too, when she could. It was my turn to protect her this time. I was thirteen, old enough to stand up to my father.

Still, I hesitated, fear dampening my bravado. I pressed my eye to the crack in the door.

Daddy shoved Mommy up against the wall with his usual violence. He buried his hand in her hair, wrenching her head back as he trapped her in place with his large body.

"Why do you make me do this, angel? You know how much I love you." His voice was low and roughened by something deeper than anger.

He crushed his lips down on hers, and Mommy moaned. For a second, I thought she was protesting, but then her hands closed around his shoulders, pulling him closer.

I watched, transfixed in my perplexity. When Daddy finally pulled away from her lips, her words shocked me to my core.

"I love you too, Roger. I'm sorry."

His hand snaked under her skirt, touching her in a forbidden place. Mommy gasped in obvious delight, her head dropping back. She kissed Daddy again.

I ran to the bathroom and vomited.

Even though nearly ten years had passed, I still shuddered at the memory. Lust made women weak, stupid. My mother had accepted my father's abuse in exchange for the flashes of pleasure he gave her. She hadn't run from his cruelty. Worst of all, she had stayed and allowed him to hurt Bea and me.

I threw myself into my studies after that, forgoing social events and rejecting boys' advances. I had one goal: to be independent. I wanted an education and a career, and I never wanted to have to depend on a man for anything. Not for money, not for emotional support, and certainly not for physical pleasure.

I told myself that I had dodged a bullet in resisting Charlie's proposal. Even though I did care for him deeply, I couldn't let go of my dream of independence.

But now that I lacked even the most basic freedoms, that sort of independence seemed laughably unattainable. I had to escape before my captor broke me completely. There had to be a way out.

I was effectively restrained, and I knew that I wasn't strong enough to fight him off if he did release me. That left one avenue for freedom: outwitting him. He had proven his intelligence, but maybe I could appeal to his human side.

If he has a shred of humanity lurking behind those evil red eyes.

I shook off the despairing thought. A defeatist attitude would all but seal my fate. I may have suffered terrible things in my lifetime, but it hadn't quashed my optimism. I had to believe that I could create a good life for myself. Otherwise, I would have withered into a pointless, empty existence long ago.

I needed a plan. Plans always made me feel better. If I had a set course of action to better my situation, then I couldn't be sucked down by hopelessness.

And my next course of action would be to discern the monster's motives for keeping me. If I knew that, then I could begin to talk him around, to make him see that he didn't really want to do this to me. I would even resort to asking a question if I had to.

Once again, I assured myself that freedom was more important than pride.

The creak of the door opening grated across my mind, shredding through my thoughts.

"Hello again, pet." The long silence of my solitude had sharpened my hearing, and his soft drawl seemed to boom around me. The shock of it made me tug against my restraints in an effort of cover my ears. His chuckle mingled with the clanking of my chains, and I cringed into the mattress.

"Are you hungry?"

His footsteps crashed down the wooden stairs, his words growing louder with his approach. It was all I could do to keep from whimpering at the assault on my eardrums.

Be polite. Be good.

If I acted compliant, maybe he would reveal his reasons for abducting me without me having to ask a question. I thought of all he had taken from me. I wasn't sure if I could bear the cost of another query.

"Yes. Master." I added the title in as meek a tone as I could manage.

I had expected his pleasure at my obedience, but instead I could practically feel his frown through the thick silence that fell over me.

"Did I… I'm sorry if I did something wrong." The tremor in my voice grated on my pride.

I'm just pretending. I'm not really worried that I upset him. A part of me acknowledged that the last part was a lie. My thighs still throbbed from his punishment, and I feared further abuse.

I pressed my legs together, an automatic attempt to protect myself. The flare of pain from the pressure on my bruises made me wince.

His fingertips trailed down my thighs in that same soothing rhythm that tormented my mind so cruelly.

"No, pet. You didn't do anything wrong. That was very good." Despite his words of approval, his tone held a thread of regret.

What did he want from me? He had demanded obedience. Was his true desire my pain, my anguish?

No. I couldn't think like that. I had to press on with my plan. With great effort, I forced the tension from my muscles, adopting a compliant façade.

My cuffs tugged at my arms as he released the tiny padlocks that secured them to my wrists. Once I was free, his arm snaked around my upper back, propping me up so that I was cradled against his chest.

"Open your mouth."

I only hesitated for a heartbeat before obeying.

Be good. I might have been freed from my restraints, but I didn't have a hope of escaping his firm hold. His hard chest and corded arms reminded me of his strength all too clearly. If I fought, he would hurt me again. That might please him, but it wouldn't help me manipulate him into releasing me.

Just as it had the first time, water dripped from his cupped hand as he brought it to my lips. It seemed the only way I would find sustenance while in captivity would be to accept it from his hands. He fed me meat this time. I accepted small chunks of it from between his fingers. It was warm and rich on my tongue, and more flavorful than anything I could recall.

When he deemed that I had eaten enough, he gave me more water. He pressed his fingers into my mouth again, forcing me to suckle him to get what I needed.

I tamped down my fury and revulsion, resolutely remaining supple in his hold.

Don't fight. Don't bite him.

"Thank you, Master." Even though the water had wet my mouth, the words spread dry ashes on my tongue.

I need him to trust me. I need him to talk to me.

His only response was a surprised grunt.

What was I doing wrong? Fearful desperation obliterated any plans for careful patience.

"Why are you doing this?"

I snapped my mouth closed so firmly that my teeth caught my cheek. Salty blood touched my tongue.

"I'm sorry," I gasped. "Please. Don't answer. Don't-"

My words were cut off by a surprised squeal when his free arm hooked beneath my knees, lifting me up. The sensation of being carried was disorienting. It momentarily robbed me of the ability to think in the wake of primal panic at the fear of falling. Instinctively, I clutched at him, my fists balling in the front of his shirt as I sought something solid to steady myself.

He didn't release his hold on my waist when he eased my legs down. My feet touched the floor. It was cold and smooth, more familiar beneath my soles than I would have expected of the rough concrete.

A shocked shout burst from me when the freezing water hit my back. I tried to run, to escape from the frigid cascade that made my skin pebble and my nerve endings scream.

His growl was harsh and forbidding, and his hands curled around my hips to hold me firmly under the spray. It occurred to me that the cold water must be hitting him, too, but his stance suggested that he held most of his body away from it.

He's standing outside the shower.

I was still blind, but my mind pieced it together.

My arms wrapped tightly around my chest in an effort to ward off the chill. Agonizing minutes passed while the water slowly grew warmer. By the time it was tepid, my teeth were chattering madly and my entire body was shaking.

His hands shifted to rub up and down my arms, pressing the warming water into my skin to alleviate the misery of the cold. I leaned into him, craving his heat.

"I'm doing this because I want to." The answer was matter-of-fact, almost detached.

The water had grown as hot as my tears by the time they began trickling down my face. My earlier suspicions were proving to be correct: he wanted my anguish more than my obedience, and he didn't possess a shred of humanity.

Once again, I was paying a steep price for a useless answer. Between the punishing cold shower and his intimate touches, this consequence promised a blend of pain and humiliation. I had no doubt he intended to push me to that pathetic state where I looked to him for comfort after his torment.

I resolved not to give in. Not again.

My resistance proved to be a pitiful thing.

His hands were slick as they ran over my skin, returning heat to my frigid flesh. The slippery soap made his calloused palms feel almost glossy as they roved over me. He began innocently enough – well, as innocent as a man violating a naked woman can manage – rubbing my arms, my shoulders. By the time he worked soap into my hair, my skin was tingling from the water's hot spray and the glorious release of tension.

How could his touch be so merciful and so ruthless at the same time?

His fingers tickled down the column of my neck, making me shiver from something other than cold. He moved downward, rubbing his palms in a circular motion as he neared my breasts. I braced myself for abuse, but he skirted around them, smoothing his hands down my sides to wash my stomach. His fingers teased the lower swell of my breasts. They suddenly felt heavier, and my nipples began to throb in an unfamiliar tempo. When he finally grazed his palms over the tightened peaks, I gasped. I only just managed to stop myself from arching into his touch.

No. My body wasn't enjoying this treatment. It couldn't.

I focused on my hatred. It bloomed white hot in my dark world, its righteous brilliance spreading throughout my being until I shook from my rage rather than in response to his touch.

I cried out when his hand gripped my sex hard, his disapproving growl vibrating against my skin. He could read me all too easily.

The fear that arose in response to that knowledge shattered my concentration, and I forgot my hatred. All that existed was the shock of his hand on the place that had never been touched so intimately, not even by me.

His fingers roughly explored my folds, rubbing soap between them. I wasn't entire sure if the slickness there was from the water that coursed down my body. I didn't dare contemplate what else it might be.

In my blindness, the humiliation of being washed and the shock of violation overwhelmed all thought.

My mind broke.

He tenderly pulled my sobbing body against his, holding me as the water cascaded over both of us. The thin material of his t-shirt was a barely perceptible barrier between us. It was sodden, plastered to him like a second skin. My body had never been so closely molded to a man's. The unfamiliarity, the foreignness of it all, only further pushed me into mindless despair.

Eventually, he deemed that I was thoroughly clean. He wrapped a soft, fluffy towel around me, hugging me to his chest as he carried me back to my bed.

I didn't even try to fight him when he secured my restraints around my wrists.

My bed. *My* restraints.

I shuddered at my mind's acceptance of my prison.

He gently removed the sodden blindfold, but my eyes didn't have time to adjust to the light before he tied a dry strip of cloth around my head.

Relief warred with regret at my prolonged blindness. Being trapped in the dark was hastening my descent into madness. I had no sense of time, no perception of the world around me.

But sight would mean seeing *his* face, so beautiful and yet so fearsome. Would his eyes shine gold or flash red as he looked down upon my nakedness?

I didn't want to know.

His Journal

May 2, 1978

> *It's been ten days since she asked her last question. When I first found her to be so sweetly obedient, I feared I would have to dispose of her sooner than I had wished. If she had truly broken so quickly, I would have grown bored of her much faster.*
>
> *When I realized it was a ploy to win my trust, I was pleased. Possibly even thrilled. I can't be sure. I've never been thrilled before. Whatever it was, I enjoyed it immensely.*
>
> *I can't decide whether I'm happy or disappointed that she hasn't asked another question since then. Emotions are unfamiliar and often seem interchangeable for me. They are all so visceral. Now that I hold her life in my hands, I have that glorious feeling of being alive all the time.*
>
> *I can say with certainty that I am more than satisfied at her resilience.*

She won't break any time soon. In a way, I don't really want her to. I might have to find a new toy if she can no longer fulfill my needs.

But for now, she only stokes my need, this lust that had always eluded me until I took her. I promised that I wouldn't rape her, and I'll stick to my word. Forcing her to ask me to fuck her will make it worth the wait. I've learned to slake myself to thoughts of her body writhing beneath me, her cries giving voice to the mix of pleasure and pain that I give her. One day, she won't know the difference between the two, just as I can hardly discern between joy and anger. My darkness will taint her, twist her into something like me. She'll be truly broken.

I'm not sure if I crave or dread the day when that will happen. It might just be the day I have to kill her.

Chapter 4

Kathleen

Why me?

What would Mary Richards do?

I laughed hollowly into the darkness. My old mantra seemed as useless as my fettered arms. Mary Richards had faced being a single career woman in a male-dominated field. She had never dealt with imprisonment and psychological torture.

For so many years, she had been my heroine. She was an independent woman who didn't need a man to create a happy, successful life for herself. When I first saw *The Mary Tyler Moore Show* at the age of fourteen, I found my role model.

Now, I had replayed every episode in my head. For a while, the Technicolor images that filled my mind helped to stave off the delirium brought on by the ever-present, crushing darkness. But joy soon gave way to obsession as I clung to the stories, playing them again and again. Then obsession had given way to anger and resentment, and I couldn't even bear to think one verse of Sonny Curtis' "Love is All Around."

I wasn't gonna make it after all.

The life I had dreamed of having in Chicago – a career in advertising and a one-bedroom apartment – was so far from my current reality that it was painful to think about.

I hadn't been allowed the luxury of sight in… Well, I didn't know how long. It felt like years, but it might have been days.

Every time I had an opportunity to glimpse him, I had wasted it out of fear. I didn't want to look up into those terrifying, mesmerizing eyes. I had precious seconds to view the world around me when He changed out my sodden blindfold for a dry one after he washed me.

In truth, the time it took him to complete that task was probably too brief for my eyes to adjust. Even the dim light burned through my eyelids in those few heartbeats when I might have gazed upon him.

Him, He. I was beginning to think of him as the only man, the only real thing in the world. He didn't have a name, but I had to have some way of thinking of him. And I refused to think of him as Master, even though I used the honorific title when He allowed me to speak a few precious words.

At first, my voice had been strong. I spoke to myself for long periods of time in order to cut through the painful silence. But I was slowly growing to hate the sound of my own voice. What good was talking if there was no one there to answer? And I didn't dare ask questions when He came to me. Conversation was impossible when the exchanges between us only allowed a brief "Yes, Master" or "No, Master" on my part. Now, moving my tongue to shape even those simple words was becoming difficult.

He never allowed me to see his face. Even though I couldn't physically read his emotions, I was beginning to fear that He was becoming bored with me.

He brought food and water to me intermittently. I could never tell if ages or no time at all had passed between those times. We followed what was now a familiar pattern: I accepted sustenance from his hand only, and He washed me. Although he touched my bare skin, he didn't violate me again; after that first time, he avoided my breasts and my sex. If He did touch them, it was a detached, dutiful thing.

I was horrified to realize that having his hands on me didn't really bother me anymore. I was completely dependent on him for every necessity, and when reduced to basic survival imperatives, my mind turned more primal. It was a struggle to maintain lucidity, to think of anything other than when He would come back, when I would feel human contact and hear a voice that was not my own.

I'm not gonna make it after all.

That single, small, defeatist thought jolted my brain back to life. I had never before allowed myself to succumb to despair. I always had a plan, was always determined to achieve my goals, no matter how hard I had to work to attain them.

It was time to speak again. It was time to ask another question.

Forming complex, coherent thoughts was a struggle at first, but I reached deep within myself, finding the steely determination that had always resided within me. I was a survivor, and I wasn't going to give in to the monster who reveled in tormenting me.

I realized that neither of us thought of the other as completely human. In my mind, he was a monster, and in his mind, I was a plaything. If I could find a way to make him see me as more than that, maybe He would begin to feel guilty about what he was doing to me. If I was a real person in his eyes, surely I could draw compassion out of him.

My mind combed through the various questions I could ask in order to get what I wanted. I had to choose carefully. All of his answers so far had proven useless, and they had cost me dearly.

He was already robbing me of my sanity, of my will to fight. What more could He take from me?

So many things, a cruel, cynical voice whispered through my consciousness.

Terrible consequences that He might inflict upon me threatened to consume my thoughts. I shoved them back. All I could focus on was my question. I couldn't forget my purpose or allow him to frighten me into silence. He hadn't hurt me physically since I had paid the price for asking who He was, but the emotional torment of this sensory deprivation was so much worse. I would almost welcome that pain.

At least I would feel *something.* Something other than his tender touches that I was coming to crave in a most perverse way. If He didn't treat me with his sadistic brand of kindness, I might have been able to hold on to my hatred in order to resist him.

My question became a litany in my head. I couldn't let go of it; I couldn't fall into thoughts of him. That path led to madness.

When the door creaked open, my body tensed in nervous anticipation. His footsteps paused on the stairs. I hadn't shown any signs of resistance in a long time.

His low chuckle was one of pleasure, and He descended the stairs more quickly than usual, as though he was eager to get to me.

The bed dipped beside me as He settled himself down onto it, but he didn't reach for my restraints. That was usually the first thing He did before gathering me up in his arms and feeding me. I realized that I had done something to break our holding pattern, and a chill swept through me.

As much as I hated the routine that was carefully designed to drive me to madness, fear of the unknown welled up, stronger than I could ever recall.

I jumped when He gently traced the line of my cheekbone.

"What are you thinking, pet?" His voice held an edge of anticipation that mirrored my own, only where mine was fearful, his was eager. My gut clenched at the sound.

"Why…" I took a deep breath to steel my resolve. I wouldn't back down now.

And a sick part of me was vaguely satisfied that He was pleased with me. My recognition of that fact was the final push I needed to follow through with my plan which would help me retain my sanity. It might even secure my freedom.

"Why me?" My voice was hoarse from disuse, but my question was discernable. All of my plotting had brought me to those two simple words. Surely a blunt question warranted a blunt answer. I hoped to compel his honesty by eliciting an automatic response.

My heart sank when He didn't answer immediately.

Oh, god. This was how it had been before. He prepared me for whatever torture he had in mind, and then he provided the answer.

Would this one be as useless as the rest?

My body began to tremble.

His thumbs hooked below the lower edge of the blindfold, and He gently eased it up over my brow. I scrunched my eyes closed, a small sound of discomfort working its way up my throat. I feared the pain of the light, and I feared to look upon his beautiful, disgusting features.

The light forcing its way through my eyelids dimmed, and his fingers stroked my cheek in that cruelly soothing motion. Tentatively, I eased my eyes open to slits. He was shading my eyes with his hand, protecting me from the harsh light until my vision could adjust.

Even the sight of his palm was breathtaking. It had been so long since I had seen anything. My eyes greedily roved over the lines etched upon it, taking note of the callouses at the base of each of his fingers.

Suddenly, I wondered what He did to get those callouses. Thus far, I had done my best to ignore the sensation of their roughness against my skin, but now they intrigued me. I knew nothing about this man who held me hostage. Understanding him might be the key to my freedom. But how could I discover anything about him if I couldn't ask questions?

Even now, I regretted the simple question I had just asked. I could tell from his demeanor that nothing good would come of it. Still, I foolishly held my breath in the hopes that He might say something of use.

When I finally blinked away the last of the pain from my burning eyes, he slowly withdrew his hand from above my eyes. For a moment, He looked glorious; He was my fallen angel.

Then horrific words dripped from his full lips, and the illusion of perfection was shattered.

"You want to know why I chose you? I took you because you were convenient."

Tears leaked from the corners of my eyes to drip down into my hair, and I turned my face away from him.

Useless. What would He make me surrender to him this time? What would He take from me in exchange for that answer? It didn't help me in any way; it didn't sway him, and it didn't yield any further information about him.

No. That was wrong. I just didn't want to accept what I had learned about him.

He was more than simply callous or selfish; He was heartless. The monster had no sense of empathy or compassion. It was as though he had no understanding of human emotion at all.

He gave me a lopsided smile, but it was nothing more than a veneer of happiness. The red glint in his eyes let me know that it was only a twisted form of pleasure. Even a beast could feel pleasure, a base satisfaction.

He lightly touched my breast in a mockery of a lover's caress.

"Now. Let's find out what makes you scream, pet." He said the words softly, almost tenderly. This was what he truly wanted: not my obedience, but my agony.

My defiance reared its head. Trapped by my restraints, there was nothing I could do to fight him physically. I quelled the urge to jerk wildly against my bonds, to allow crushing fear to overwhelm my mind. My mind was my only weapon, and I wouldn't give it up so easily.

Lifting my chin, I stared directly into his glowing amber eyes.

I will not scream for him. Not this time.

My challenging glare elicited a grin from my tormentor. He chuckled down at me almost affectionately.

"You won't break any time soon, will you?" He tapped his finger against my forehead. "My clever pet."

The words made my stomach turn, but I realized that I had learned something else about him. He might have taken me because I was convenient, but I was important to him in some capacity. If I didn't know better, I would say he was growing… fond of me.

If He enjoyed my defiance, then I would give it to him. That suited my tastes just fine. If he truly was feeling some affection for me, I needed to foster that. If he cared, he might feel guilty about what he was doing to me. He might let me go.

Suddenly, He grabbed my breasts with punishing force. I bit my tongue to keep from crying out. I was becoming immune to the shame of his touch upon my naked flesh, but he hadn't truly hurt me since I had asked him why he was doing this to me.

"Has anyone ever touched you here, pet?" His long drawl was a low rumble. He released one of my breasts, and his hand closed roughly around my sex. "How about here?"

I might have been fooling myself, but I imagined that his grip was a touch possessive. Another point in my favor.

Despite the tiny spark of triumph within me, my cheeks flamed with my embarrassment. When He had washed me, his touches had been impersonal. This was entirely different. He wanted to know my secrets. He wanted to take ownership of these forbidden parts of me.

He threw back his head and laughed, reading me easily. The sound was one of pure, perverse glee. It was a tangible force, clinging to my skin with toxic joy.

"Is my pet a virgin?"

Two fingers teased between my lower lips, threatening to push into my opening. I clenched against the invasion, and a twinge of pain hit me when He met the barrier of my tightened muscles.

For a moment, his ruthless expression made me fear that He would force his way in, tearing into me. Instead, he retreated slightly, his touch playing through my folds.

"I asked you a question," He said on a low growl, his grip tightening threateningly.

I clenched my jaw, refusing to allow the affirmation of his suspicions to pass through my lips. It was too personal, too humiliating. I wasn't ashamed of the fact that I was untouched. But it was a part of my identity. I was Kathleen Marie White, and I had denied men again and again in my dedication to my independence.

The monster wanted to take that from me, and if I allowed that, He would take another piece of my self, my soul.

I had a moment to register his frown at my reticence before the pain hit. Fire bloomed between my legs, turning to a harsh sting on my labia. My legs closed tightly, instinct driving me to apply pressure to alleviate the fire.

He clucked his tongue as though at a disobedient child and settled his weight over my knees, stretching me open. My muscles quivered, futilely straining to escape his hold.

"Answer me." The order was a calm demand. "Are you a virgin?"

His hand came down again.

"Yes!" The word left my lips on a strangled shout. This was far worse than when He had slapped my legs. It was as though my intimate flesh was ten times more sensitive than my tender thighs. The stinging barbs of hundreds of bees pierced my skin.

Another hit. "Address me properly, pet."

"Yes, Master! Please. Please stop!"

I tensed when his hand moved toward my sex once again, then sobbed in relief when He did nothing more than firmly press his palm against me. I couldn't help pushing up into him, desperate for the pressure and heat that would help override the cruel sting.

"I'm going to learn your body, pet. And I suspect I'll teach you a few things in the process. I won't stop until you scream for me."

He'll stop when I scream? I can oblige him.

I let out a piercing wail, flinging my fury and frustration and hatred at him. My eyes glared daggers into his.

He slapped me again, and this time my scream was genuine.

I blinked through the tears clouding my vision to find him frowning down at me. It wasn't an angry frown, but one of mild reproval.

"That scream was a lie, and I won't tolerate dishonesty. I am always honest with you. Do you value your questions?" There was a knowing gleam in his eye. "I know you plan them, carefully parsing them out when you're desperate to know more. I can take that from you. And then I can take everything from you. Do you understand me?"

Oh, I understood. Terror gripped me at my understanding. If He chose to end our game, I could no longer control how much I gave up to him.

He could rape me, beat me, inflict whatever horrors that pleased him upon me.

"Y-Yes." I swallowed hard. "I understand, Master."

His thumbs brushed the tears from my cheeks.

"Besides, that's not the kind of screaming I had in mind. You earned that pain just now, but that's not your consequence for your question. That was discipline."

Oh, god. The torment hadn't even begun? More tears slipped over his thumbs.

He cupped my face in one hand and trailed his fingers down my throat. It elicited a tickling sensation, but my shiver wasn't an unpleasant one. He traced the shell of my ear. When he gently tugged on my lobe, there was a strange stirring between my legs.

"What-?" I stopped myself just in time. *What are you doing to me?*

He knew what I was going to ask. "I'm exploring you, pet. I want to find out what makes you tick. What makes you scream."

What makes you scream. I understood now; He wanted me to scream in ecstasy. Horror rolled through me, but it didn't entirely dampen the heat that He was stoking low in my belly with his gentle touches.

I couldn't help it; I jerked at my restraints. "Please. Don't."

He abruptly shifted to tweak my nipple. It was a hard peak, and the little twist of pain He gave me was echoed by the clenching of my inner walls.

"Please." My plea was a low whine, and it wasn't entirely one of physical distress.

His lips were only a hairsbreadth from my throat, and his warm breath teased across my sensitized flesh when He chuckled against me.

"I knew we would get along, pet."

He kept one hand at my breast, toying with my nipple. He pinched it and then rolled it between his thumb and forefinger, easing the pain to a dull ache before giving me another little bite of pain. The ache kept a warm buzz building between my legs, and each pinch made my inner walls flutter.

His other hand glided down my stomach, pausing to tease the upper edge of my soft curls. The heat of his fingers seemed to seep through my skin to my womb. A sheen of sweat broke out on my skin, and a different wetness began to gather between my labia.

What is happening to me?

Charlie had never made me feel anything like this. I had been right to keep him from touching me. Just as I had feared, my body was weak. Lust was a weapon, and my captor wielded it cruelly.

"I hate you," I hissed out through gritted teeth.

He just gave me a sardonic smile. His touch explored lower, and his fingers found a hardened bud nestled in my curls. Pleasure rolled over me when He brushed over it.

His smile widened, and He pressed his thumb against me, rubbing in firm circles.

"Do you hate me now?"

"Yes." The word was a moan.

He caught the bud between his fingers, squeezing hard. My eyes flew open and a little shocked cry shot out. Pain flared, but so did the heat within me.

"What have I told you about addressing me with proper respect?" He asked calmly as He tightened his grip, twisting my nipple at the same time.

A line of white-hot fire connected the two abused areas.

"Yes, Master!"

But I could no longer remember what question I was answering. Sensation assaulted every fiber of my being, swirling in my mind. The pleasure and pain mingled together in an intoxicating cocktail.

When his finger found my secret opening again, the folds were swollen and wet beneath his touch. He began to press into me, and my fear flared. My eyes flew wide, beseeching.

"No! Please."

I tried to clench my thighs together, to block his intrusion. His weight on my knees held me open.

"It's all right, pet," He practically cooed. "Let me in. You'll like it."

Those maddening circles around my clitoris increased, and He took my entire breast in his hand, massaging it. I couldn't help arching into him with a gasp, and his finger slid into me up to his first knuckle before I could stop him again. It took effort. I was slick, and my core was burning, craving… something.

His finger began to pump in and out, making shallow forays into me while his thumb continued to wring pleasure from me. Slowly, He eased his way in, until his palm was flush with my sex.

"No." The whispered word was ragged, and it held no real conviction. My brain was flooded with pleasure, and coherent thought was becoming difficult to maintain. All I knew was that I should be protesting for some reason. I shouldn't want this.

Then his finger crooked inside me, rubbing against the front wall of my core. The pleasurable sensation magnified to an unbearable degree when He found a secret spot there. My muscles quivered around Him uncontrollably, and my eyes rolled back in my head on a moan.

No. But my hips rolled wantonly beneath Him, my back arching up to press my breast into his hand.

I wanted… I wanted…

He pinched my nipped cruelly, twisting hard.

I exploded, my entire body quaking as ecstasy I had never known before slammed through me.

He pumped in and out of me, relentlessly stimulating the spot that was making me come undone.

"That's it, pet. Good girl." His cajoling praise mingled with my delighted scream.

My body was still shaking when He gently withdrew from me. The light in his eyes was feverish, gold glinting through the red, and his twisted smile was back in place. His chest was heaving with excitement, his breathing almost as harsh as mine.

As my mind slowly coalesced, shame gathered in my chest, making me shudder with revulsion rather than pleasure.

I had yearned to make him see me as more than a plaything, but I would never be more than his toy. Suddenly, the endearment *pet* seemed generous. At least it indicated that He saw me as a living thing.

No. That was wrong. He wasn't being generous. There was no satisfaction to be found in breaking something that couldn't fight back, that couldn't feel pain or anguish.

I wept in longing to be his toy rather than his pet. I didn't want to be conscious of the feel of his sensual hands upon me, of the mental torment elicited by the pleasure He harvested from me.

I'm not his pet. I'm a woman. I'm Kathleen. Kathleen Marie White.

Kathleen Marie White wanted to die.

His Journal

May 12, 1978

*I saw something shatter in her eyes
when she came apart under my
hands that first time. She was so
beautiful.*

Man, I want to fuck her.

*We've returned to our usual routine
where I feed and bathe her. And
now I get to touch her.*

*I always visit her at irregular
intervals. I'm fairly certain there's
no way she has any sense of time
while I keep her blindfolded, but
keeping her on a set schedule might
help her perceive the passage of
time.*

*But now I get to see her more often.
I have a hard time stopping myself
from spending hours playing with
her. I'm learning how to touch her
in just the right way to make her
orgasm. She leans into my touch*

now rather than shying away. I wonder if she realizes?

Her life depends on food and water and flashes of ecstasy. Her life depends on me.

It's heady knowledge, but her body tempts me. I don't like that.

I want to take her so badly, to bury myself inside her tight, wet heat. When she writhes beneath me, her cunt clenching around my fingers, I almost lose control. I promised not to rape her, but I don't give a shit about honesty. Keeping my word is about maintaining the balance of power. If I fuck her before she asks for it, she'll know that she holds some sort of feminine power over me.

If I want to maintain absolute control of her, I have to control myself.

Chapter 5

Kathleen

Will you ever let me go?

You're sick. You're perverted. You're fundamentally wrong.

My thoughts weren't directed at him; they were directed towards myself. In the time that had passed since I had experienced my first orgasm by his hand, my self-loathing had increased one hundred fold. How could I possibly find such perfect ecstasy when I was being touched against my will?

Was it against my will?

If I was honest with myself – a practice that was growing almost too painful to bear – I recognized that I was coming to anticipate his touch. The anticipation had been nervous, fearful at first. But now I couldn't deny that it had morphed into something resembling eagerness.

He didn't pleasure me every time He came to me, and the last time He had left after feeding me, I had shamefully whimpered my protest.

My only comfort was the knowledge that I wasn't alone in my longing. When He settled his body above mine, pinning me in place, his own arousal was blatantly obvious. He gave me pleasure while denying himself.

If I could tempt him to take me, that would give me some power over him. If I could enthrall him with my body, maybe he would soften towards me; maybe I could make him care. If He cared about me, He might let me go.

Yes. That's it. I don't actually want him to touch me. I'm pretending so that he'll lose control and take me. That will give me the upper hand.

The words rang false in my own mind, but they were all I had.

It wasn't as though I was unfamiliar with a man's arousal. I had never tried to tempt Charlie, but it had happened often enough anyway.

Charlie.

I had all but forgotten about my almost-fiancé. Now I dug into those memories. They had once filled me with shame and confusion, but now I viewed them as a useful tool. What had I done to make Charlie harden against me? To make him beg to get inside me?

"Kathleen, baby. Please. I'm dying here." Charlie's groan was saturated with deepest need, and I knew that he wasn't just saying it to manipulate me into letting him have me.

He was lying atop me, our bodies awkwardly entwined in the backseat of his Mustang. His lips tasted of Pabst Blue Ribbon, and the earthy tang of marijuana was steeped into the upholstery beneath me.

I didn't mind that Charlie smoked and drank, but I didn't touch the stuff. It made people weak, dulled their consciousness. I had to stay sharp or I might lose control.

Especially when I was pinned under Charlie, his mouth caressing mine. If I was intoxicated, I might give in to him. Not out of my own arousal – I never felt the same stirring in my loins that affected him so deeply – but out of a sense of guilt.

Charlie was truly a good guy, and a foxy one at that. I could hardly believe that he had chosen me, the plain prude. I wanted to give him what he desired because I cared about him.

His hips ground against mine, and his hardness prodded pleadingly at my belly. He released my lips so that he could stare down into my eyes. His were a gorgeous, shocking blue that threatened to make me melt if I dwelled on how beautiful they were. He tenderly brushed my hair back from my brow.

"Please, baby. I won't hurt you. I would never hurt you."

"I know," I admitted tremulously. "But I can't-"

"You can trust me Kathleen. I want to spend forever with you. You know I don't want anyone else."

I blinked up at him. "Why?" I asked softly, truly at a loss.

"You're smart and driven and beautiful. You're the strongest woman I've ever met. I'll spend forever with you because I love you, Kathleen."

It was the first time he had ever said that. His eyes were so open and earnest that it made my heart hurt. It would have been so much easier if he had been lying to get into my pants.

I turned my face away, no longer able to look into those gorgeous eyes.

"I'm sorry. I can't." I wasn't sure if I was telling him I couldn't sleep with him or I couldn't love him.

I shook off the sadness of the memory and the anguish at thinking of my life before my imprisonment. I had to focus. What had I been doing that had so enflamed Charlie's lust?

I had been kissing him, nothing more.

Kissing my captor was definitely out of the question. It was a loving, intimate act, and although He touched me in intimate places, the emotional bond of true intimacy was utterly absent. A man without emotions couldn't even begin to understand that.

So how was it that my body came alive under his touch in a way it never had for Charlie?

He abuses you.

I shuddered in revulsion. Did I truly enjoy what He did to me because of my dark past? Had that memory of my mother being abused and aroused by my father tainted me forever?

God, no.

That couldn't be right. Bea had found a kind, caring man to marry. Despite the fact that my sister had grown up in the same shitty household as I had, she seemed to have maintained normality when it came to sex.

Thinking of my sister was even more painful than thinking about Charlie. I hated my memories of my life outside my prison, my life in the light.

But those memories might hold the keys to finding that light again. If I could manage to manipulate him sexually, I might be able to convince him to release me.

I thought back to the worst fight I had ever shared with my sister.

"Bea, don't be an idiot!" I half-shrieked, fear for my sister warring with my frustration with her. "You can't marry John. You're too young to be a wife."

"Don't tell me what I can't do!" She flung back at me, her pale green eyes flaring beneath her brunette bangs. The freckles dusting her nose made her appear shockingly young.

But her words were more formidable than any child's ever could be. "God, Kathleen, you're just like Dad. I'm eighteen. I'm a woman now, and I can do whatever I want with my life."

"I am nothing *like Dad." My eyes narrowed to slits at the cutting accusation. "I'm just trying to help you, Bea. Can't you see that? You have to go to college. You don't have to rely on a man to escape this house." I gestured at the peeling walls that had been the borders of our hell for so many years. "If you marry John, he'll expect you to sleep with him. He'll be able to control you."*

Her cold laugh was like a slap in the face. "Do you really think I'm a dork like you?" She asked, her voice mocking. "I'm not a virgin, idiot.

I've already slept with John. I'm going to marry him because I love him, not because I'm fucking him."

My hands clenched to fists at my sides, my fingernails biting into my palms. "You idiot! You only think you love him because you've had sex with him!"

Mustering up my willpower, I reined in my anger. Bea was my little sister. It was my job to take care of her. "Don't do this, Bea. Let me help you. I can write your college applications. I can-"

"Don't you dare," Bea hissed. "You're always talking about being independent and making your own choices. Well, this is my choice. I choose John."

Sex had obviously messed with my sweet sister's brain. She married John a month later, and her belly swelled with a baby only a few months after that. I had lost her to lust.

Could I make my tormentor lose himself to lust? Or would I lose myself, as I had always feared?

My mad giggle cut through the dark silence. I was already losing myself. I could barely recall my life before my captivity without exerting great effort.

I was desperate enough to roll the dice.

I'll just pretend. I'll pretend I like it when he touches me. Then he'll take me, and he'll be the weak one.

I licked my lips as He removed the blindfold. My nervousness made them dry. Or maybe I was already putting my plan to seduce Him in motion.

His eyes fixated on my mouth, following the movement of my darting tongue. That lopsided smile twisted his lips again. The sight of it made my stomach turn and my sex clench. It also made hope swell within my chest. He was affected by signs of my arousal.

His smirk turned down into a frown, and a fine line appeared between His brows. He touched His fingers to the corner of my mouth, and I realized my mistake: my lips had quirked up at the corners in satisfaction.

"Why the smile, pet?" His voice was quiet, but there was a threat laced through the whisper. "Are you truly happy to see me? Or do you want something else?"

Panic slammed into me. My emotions were wild, unwieldy after spending so much time in silent, blind isolation. He had always been able to read me easily, but now I was so raw that my feelings showed plainly on my face.

"No, Master. I mean, yes," I babbled. "I'm happy to see you, Master."

I licked my lips again, hoping to glimpse that spark of interest in his eyes. Instead, they flared with disapproval, anger, even. It was the most emotion I had ever seen in him.

Hope had a moment to tentatively form within me once again. Through using my sexuality, I had at least gotten him to feel *something*.

Within seconds, the emotion drained from his features, replaced by his satisfied half-smile.

Without a word, He reached for the blindfold and secured it over my eyes.

I expected to hear the *snick* of my cuffs being unlocked, as He usually did before He fed me; I already knew He wasn't going to touch me this time. I had failed.

Instead, my ears were met with the sound of his retreating footsteps.

Oh, god.

If He left now, would He ever come back? Had I crossed some invisible line, and He was done with me? Was He just going to leave me here to die?

"Please." I had to force the word out of my seizing lungs. "Please don't leave me here."

The first stair squealed beneath his weight.

"No!" I cried, desperate. I was terrified of dying in the dark, horrified at the knowledge that the madness would claim me long before my body finally expired. "Please don't leave me, Master!"

He continued his steady progress up the stairs. I twisted against my bonds, fighting more furiously than I had since my first days of captivity.

"Please. If you - don't want me - anymore - let me go. Don't – Don't leave me here." I was hyperventilating, and my words came out on ragged gasps. "Please. Let me - go. Will you - ever - let me - go?"

His footsteps stopped.

My mouth snapped closed.

A question. I had asked a question. I had been so careful for so long, but my fear of death was going to destroy me. He might allow me to live, but by the time He finished with me, I wouldn't really be *alive.*

Dread curled in my gut as I listened to his approach. I wanted to beg him not to answer, to ignore my question, but that hadn't stopped him before. Sobs wracked my entire body by the time He sank down on the mattress beside me.

His thumbs brushed away the wetness on my cheeks with a familiar, cruel tenderness. I whimpered beneath him, my body trembling with my delirious panic.

He lifted the blindfold from my eyes, but I kept them closed tight. He smoothed the creases in my brow with a gentle touch.

"Shhh, pet. I'm not angry, and I won't hurt you. Not this time. You've pleased me. You're so beautiful when you beg."

Beautiful. On someone else's lips, the word might have been sweet. On his, it was a revolting parody of a compliment.

"And no. I will never let you go."

No. That couldn't be true. I refused to believe it. I had lasted so long, had been trying so hard...

He gripped my chin, stilling the unconscious shaking of my head. His eyes blazed like red-gold flames.

"I will never let you go," he told me again, more firmly this time. The words were almost... fervent.

He cares about me. He cares. He has to. Despite his declaration, his expression gave me a spark of hope. If he cared about me, he might release me from his cruel bondage.

He studied me for a long moment, and his pleased grin lit up his breathtaking features.

"You don't believe me. You still think you can win." He stroked my hair tenderly. "You don't know how…" He seemed to fumble for a word. "*Happy* you make me, pet."

I knew better. His smile held no true happiness; he was incapable of such an emotion. But there was more feeling behind his eyes than there had been before.

Wasn't there?

I make him happy. He cares.

If he cared about me, he wouldn't hurt me anymore. Would he?

His pleased chuckle rolled over me, and he tapped my nose with something resembling affection.

"Maybe you'll believe me by the time you've paid the price for your question. Maybe not." He cocked his head at me, considering. "I hope not."

My mind was a tangle. Instinct told me to defy him. But how could I defy him when his wishes aligned with my own? I didn't want to believe that He wouldn't let me go. I couldn't allow myself to believe that. But He wanted me to deny his words; He enjoyed the fact that I remained unbroken. I was still whole enough for him to play with me.

I didn't want to be broken, but I also didn't want to do what He wanted. How should I feel when He didn't want me to be broken?

My frustration escaped me on a wordless shout, and I jerked at my restraints. I wanted to lash out at him, to claw at those beautiful eyes.

He continued to stroke my hair. His smile might have been confused for sweetness. "You're very cute when you're angry, pet." Suddenly, his fingers were at my clit, pinching lightly, bringing it to life. "But you're beautiful when you beg."

He wanted me to beg him to stop touching me?

Fuck you! I didn't dare speak the crass words aloud, but my eyes conveyed my hatred, my defiance.

If he wanted me to beg him to stop, I would allow myself to revel in his touch. He had proven to me time and again that he could wring pleasure from my body despite my mind's wishes. I couldn't think of a more effective way to beat him at his own game than cooperating.

I dimly noted that everything was becoming twisted, and my actions were becoming just the opposite of what they should be. But I was too fixated on my ire to contemplate that.

I walked right into his trap.

My hips rolled up into his touch, and I closed my eyes, honing in on the pleasure that was pulsating outward from my rapidly hardening clit. Recognizing my arousal, He pinched the bud. I gasped and writhed beneath him as my sex clenched in response.

"My pet likes a bite of pain, doesn't she?"

I realized too late that the pain wasn't meant to be a punishment, but a reward. I didn't understand. Didn't He want me to beg for him to stop?

So long as I focused on the pleasure coursing through me, I wouldn't even consider begging for his touches to cease, painful or not.

I would beat him this time.

Two fingers teased through my wet folds, his thumb never leaving my clit. I thrust my hips forward, seeking to be filled.

He pulled back just enough to maintain contact without entering me, and He tweaked my nipple in reprimand.

"Not yet, greedy girl."

I would have been ashamed of my beseeching whine if I hadn't been so focused on chasing the pleasure. My hips stilled on instinct. Somewhere deep within me, I knew that He wouldn't enter me until I stopped trying to draw him in.

Control. He craved control. He thought He was controlling me by wringing pleasure from me against my will, but what He didn't realize was that it wasn't against my will this time. As soon as I came, I would throw my victory in his face. I would let him know that I had beaten him at his own game.

I made my body go supple, compliant. He rumbled his approval and eased his fingers inside. He moved in small, teasing forays, penetrating me incrementally. It took all my effort not to rock against him. I needed to come soon to make my victory all the more obvious. I would welcome my orgasm, and He would know that I had my own sense of control.

Then He touched that glorious spot inside me, and I threw myself into the ecstasy that He elicited. My body tensed, bracing for my release.

He stopped rubbing me; his sheathed fingers stilled, and his thumb left my clit.

I cried out in shocked protest, my eyes flying open to find his.

In that moment, my stomach dropped, and tears stung at the corners of my eyes.

I had lost.

He didn't want me to beg him to stop. He wanted me to beg for him to continue. He wanted me to plead for my orgasm. And I had chased my pleasure too hard now; even my hatred couldn't hold back the inevitable. He was going to keep me on this precipice, torturing me until I finally broke.

He grinned – glorying in my defeat – as He saw the knowledge bloom in my own eyes.

I had willingly, eagerly, given him my body. What I thought was an act of defiance was what He had truly desired all along.

Even as tears began to roll down my face, bliss surged within me as his fingers began to move within me once again.

I clenched my teeth together, fighting the pleasure. But He brought me to the edge again and again, only to stop just as my sex began to clutch at him.

I broke when he bit my nipple. He had never touched me with his mouth before. The pain of his bite held a strange intimacy. It pushed me over the edge.

"Please!" I let out on a ragged, desperate moan. He nipped at me again, sending heat shooting to that sweet spot between my legs, but his fingers didn't stimulate it. It wasn't enough.

"Tell your Master what you want, pet."

"I want to come!" I wept with the intensity of my need. "Please, Master-"

Any further pleading was cut off by my harsh scream as He shoved into me, fucking me hard with his fingers. At the same time, his teeth sank into my nipple. All of his gentleness was gone. I was taken, ravaged.

I reveled in it.

His Journal

May 19, 1978

> *She will beg me for my cock soon. She has to. I can't resist her for much longer. It was all I could do to stop myself from driving into her cunt when she begged me to allow her to come.*
>
> *Power. Control.*
>
> *God, she's sweet. I don't know how I lived all those years without knowing this joy. And it is joy. I recognize that now. She's helped me to understand its true meaning.*
>
> *She is powerless, restrained in the dark. She lives for me, for my touch. Her efforts to outwit me only make me crave her that much more.*
>
> *She's not broken. Not yet. I get to play with her for a while longer.*

Chapter 6

Kathleen

Why are you doing this?

Master. He had mastered my body, and now He was taking my mind. Since our last clash of wills, I had simply started to accept the pleasure He gave me. I no longer felt disgust or anger; He had broken me of that, liberated me from it when He had forced me to beg for my orgasm.

Now I accepted his touches with something between resignation and eagerness. I called him Master without a thought. He was in control of my pleasure, and there was no point fighting Him when it came to that. No matter how I fought Him, no matter how I tried to outsmart Him, he knew. He always knew. He was always ten steps ahead of me.

He was slowly chipping away at everything that made me *me.*

Kathleen Marie White. Not pet.

My hatred of my captor had begun to turn in on itself, redirecting towards me. He didn't hurt me; He wasn't torturing me into submission. Not really. Lust was making me forget who I was, just as I had always feared it would.

"You're smart and driven and beautiful. You're the strongest woman I've ever met."

Charlie had said those words to me. He had said them when I was denying him in his desire to touch my body.

That wasn't an option with my Master. He kept me restrained. I couldn't fight Him off when He touched me, and saying "no" only seemed to further enflame Him. I noticed how his hard cock throbbed against me while He tormented me.

He wanted me, and my only power lay in my denial of Him. So long as I didn't ask another question, He wouldn't have sex with me. I was coming to understand Him well enough to know that. He was too obsessed with maintaining control. He wouldn't ruin his game by breaking the rules. If He broke the rules, that meant I would have broken Him.

I had hoped that my waning resistance would goad Him into crossing that line. Even in my defeat, I still kept a spark of defiance. My mind still secretly sought ways to circumvent his control.

Despite everything He had put me through, my mind was still my own. Mostly. He might have bent me, but he hadn't broken me.

Not yet. An insidious voice that sounded suspiciously like my Master's whispered through my mind.

I slapped it away. I would never escape Him if I gave in to that voice. My only power was my mind, and although He had overcome that power with his own formidable mind time and again, I couldn't just give up.

It was time for another question. Only, this one was carefully crafted to force a more useful answer. I knew He would lie; He had lied before. I just hadn't known it then. And He might not have known it, either.

I knew the price for my question, but I was willing to pay it. How different could his cock be from his fingers? He had already violated every inch of me.

I settled into my darkness, allowing my mind to float in nothingness until He came for me. I needed to conserve my mental reserves for when I would challenge Him.

When He came to me, I said nothing while He cared for me in our usual routine. It wasn't unusual for me to remain silent, but something about the tension in my body let Him know that things were different.

Once He was finished feeding me, He removed my blindfold. Keeping me cradled in his arms, He tenderly traced the line of my lower lip.

"What do you want to say to me, pet?" Anticipation practically vibrated through Him. He knew what was coming, what He would finally be able to take from me.

I took a deep breath before uttering the words that would seal my fate.

"Why are you doing this?"

He frowned, obviously disappointed in me. "You've already asked that. I'm doing this because I want to."

"No." The denial was sharp on my tongue, definitive. This wasn't a weak protest.

His brows rose, and the disappointment etched in his features gave way to curiosity.

"No?" I expected his tone to come out low and dangerous in response to my defiance, but if anything it held the warmth of pleasure.

He's pleased that my mind hasn't broken, I realized.

I didn't care for the idea that I had pleased Him, but I didn't want to be broken, either. Ignoring the conflicting emotions that arose within me, I pressed on.

"You're lying." My declaration only slightly shook with my fear. "You don't want to do this to me."

"Oh, pet," He laughed. "You think I don't want to keep you any longer? Do you think I care about you?"

His mocking words hit close to home, and I flinched. I had hoped that his amusement with me, his pleasure at my resilience, was growing into a kind of twisted affection.

"No." I clung to my determination, gathering the few vestiges of courage that remained within my soul. "You *need* to do this to me."

His face went completely blank for the space of a moment.

He blinked.

When He looked down at me, there was respect and a hint of something akin to wonder in his eyes. Something else flashed behind them. Could it be pain?

Then his frown returned, and his fingers flexed around my arm where He held me to his chest.

"Very well, pet," he allowed, his voice tight. "I do need to do this to you. But make no mistake," his eyes burned down into mine, "I want to do this, too. I enjoy torturing you. And now, I finally get to take what I want."

It was far from a heartening response, but He suddenly showed more emotion than ever before. It manifested in a new ferocity; the restraint He had exercised for so long was utterly gone.

He shoved me back onto the bed. To my surprise, He didn't bind me with my cuffs as He usually did before He pleasured me. He didn't need them. The strong grip of his hand around my wrists, pinning them above me, was more than enough to hold me in place for Him.

His movements were frenzied, almost fumbling, as He reached into his pocket with his free hand. I recognized the small item He held as a condom in the seconds it took him to free himself from his low-slung jeans and sheathe himself.

Still fully clothed, He settled his body over mine and pressed at my entrance. I was tight with lack of arousal. He hadn't taken the time to prepare me, and the slickness I needed to accommodate him was absent.

For a moment, I feared He was going to shove in ruthlessly, but He reached between us with a growl, pinching and rubbing my clit until I began to relax. When his fingers found the wetness between my labia, He grunted in satisfaction.

The head of his cock pressed at me. It was much wider than his two fingers, and I gasped. Were all men so large? His cock had to be at least nine inches long. I tried to squirm away from Him, my body fearing the penetration.

His feral snarl warned me to stillness. He stroked my clit again, and I softened beneath Him.

Slowly, He eased into me. His breath puffed in and out in hard hisses through his teeth. I was amazed to realize that He was restraining himself from slamming into me. Did He care about not hurting me? Or was this all about his control over himself?

A second later, I decided I didn't care. He hit a barrier, and pain shot through my womb.

My hymen.

"Hold on, pet," he ground out.

His hips thrust upward, destroying my virginity. I screamed as it tore.

He released his hold on my wrists to cup my face in both hands. His forehead rested on mine, and the flames of his eyes threatened to burn right through me to scorch my soul.

It's his first time, too, I realized with a jolt.

Without thinking, I reached up to run my fingers through his hair. He leaned into my hand. It was the first time I had ever touched Him of my own volition.

"It's okay, Master," I heard myself reassuring him. "I'm okay."

His groan was one of relief, and He began to move inside me once again. Now that both of his hands were free, He was able to play with my breasts while He toyed with my clit. He gave me the little flashes of pain that I was coming to love so much, and I softened to accommodate Him further.

The agony that I had felt at his initial penetration faded, and I found myself rocking my hips up to meet Him. My hands wrapped around his shoulders. When the head of his cock found that sweet spot inside me, my fingernails bit into his skin in an effort to hold Him to me. But He wouldn't have pulled away even if I had been clawing at his eyes rather than his back.

He grasped both of my nipples between his thumb and forefinger and twisted hard. The shock of pain slammed me into my orgasm. Just as my inner walls began contracting around Him, his ecstatic shout joined mine. His cock pumped within me, matching the fluttering of my core.

I felt more alive than I had since He had abducted me. For the first time in I didn't know how long, I was connected to another human being. Maybe for the first time ever.

And He *was* human. A swell of emotion that I had never seen in Him blazed out of his eyes: a mixture of bliss and possessiveness. The lines of his face were ferocious, but He had never seemed more truly content.

I moaned as He pulled out of me, and a sudden sense of stark emptiness washed over me. Tears rolled down my face, but for once they weren't born of pain or shame. The swell of emotion within me was just as strong as his. It was so overwhelming that it made me weep.

He shifted his body so that He was resting beside me. Wrapping his arms around me, He pulled me into his chest. Without a thought, I nestled into Him. My tears wet his t-shirt, but He didn't seem to mind. I noticed that He smelled good, like salt and earth and something purely masculine that was unique to Him.

For once, the feel of his powerful muscles surrounding me didn't fill me with fear. I felt protected, comforted, treasured. The way He stroked my hair wasn't condescending or manipulative; it was a show of genuine affection.

Wasn't it?

I shut off my busy brain before it could ruin this blissful moment between us. Somewhere deep inside Him, there was a shred of humanity, and it had taken lust to pull it out of Him. I had always thought lust to be a loathsome source of weakness, but I had been wrong.

Lust was cleansing. It brought me pure joy after my endless, dark misery, and it brought out the best in Him.

I breathed in his scent and released it on a happy little sigh. His arms tightened around me, pulling me closer.

Before either of us realized what was happening, we fell asleep in each other's arms.

His Journal

May 20, 1978

*I held her because I had to. The act
of caring is essential in maintaining
control over her. She needs to crave
my cock, to beg me for it. I'll settle
for nothing less.*

*She's mine, and I intend to keep it
that way. If she breaks, she won't be*
her *anymore. And I'm enjoying her
far too much to allow that to happen.
I don't think I would like it if she
broke completely. I would have to
get rid of her, and I like the pleasure
she gives me too much to give it up.*

*I can always get another toy when
she breaks, but I don't want that. I
want her. My pretty, clever little pet.*

*As much as I enjoy her sharp mind,
I'm sometimes annoyed by how
perceptive she is. Yesterday, she
managed to truly surprise me for the
first time. When she asked me why I
was doing this to her, I was
disappointed. I thought her mind*

had finally shattered. Then she forced me to admit the truth, not only to her, but to myself.

I need to do this to her. When I abducted her, I was so fascinated with the sensation of wanting that I didn't think much beyond it. I wanted her, so I took her.

But she's right: I need to do this to her to keep the darkness from encroaching.

~~But I don't need her. Any woman would do.~~

So long as she remains with me, my needs will be met. Now that I've had a taste of her cunt, I want more.

She thinks I need her? I need to hurt her. I'll teach her to like it. She'll last longer that way.

Chapter 7

Kathleen

Why do you need to control me?

I awoke to my usual darkness. I was back in my cuffs, and the blanket covered my nakedness. I would have preferred his warmth beside me. In the time we laid in each other's embrace, we had been more than sadistic captor and desperate captive. We had been a man and a woman, tied together by the sweet bond of lust.

Lust is good. Why had I spent so many years fighting it?

Lust wasn't a weapon; it wasn't weakness. It was bliss, peace, communion. It was humanity at its most basic, the most primal form of goodness.

If that goodness hid within Him, there must be some reason it had been buried. I yearned to know more about Him, and I acknowledged that my desire wasn't entirely born of my efforts to escape him. Learning more about Him had long been a stratagem for winning my freedom. Now, it was more than that.

Yes, I did hope He would release me from this cruel bondage if I could make Him realize how much He cared. And He *did* care. No matter what his lips said, I saw it in his eyes as He moved within me in the most intimate way possible.

If that capacity for caring lurked within him, there must be some reason why it was buried so deep. What happened to Him that left Him so broken?

What made my dark angel fall?

No. He's not my angel. He's my demon, even if he does give me pleasure and the illusion of tenderness.

I had another question. After our moment of exquisite shared passion, I didn't fear Him as much as I had. I wasn't as afraid to risk asking. A sick part of me even anticipated coupling with him again. He would come to realize that the sensation He felt each time He took me was an emotional connection.

He cares. I just have to make Him see it.

I sighed, settling into my darkness until He returned and made the world materialize again. When I heard his approach, my heart leapt and my brain whirred back to life. It was as though I entered some sort of stasis when He was absent; I was only alive when He was with me.

"Hello, pet." I could hear the smile in his voice before He removed my blindfold.

His pleased grin was dazzling as ever. It had once elicited fear and anger, but now it only awoke a warm glow in my chest. That realization made me uncomfortable, but it did nothing to lessen the warmth.

It was more imperative than ever that I convince Him to let me go. My mind was fracturing, turning against me as my body had long ago. If I could help heal Him, He might not need me anymore. He would free me.

"Why do you need to control me?" I asked without preamble, not wanting to wait another second to discover his secrets.

His smile wavered, diminished by surprise. I had caught Him off guard. His forefinger hooked beneath my chin, tilting my head back so He could study my face. Heat flared in me with just that one touch. He was the only real thing in my world, and I craved Him.

Dimly, I hated that.

His lips twisted into that cruelly beautiful smile of his, but I could detect a new warmth behind it. The pleasure there wasn't simply for my anguish.

I wasn't anguished. Not really. Not while He was touching me. I was enthralled.

And so was He.

"Eager for more already, pet?" He asked with soft satisfaction. "You'll get more than my cock for that question."

Fear fluttered to life in my belly, emanating through my disconcerting contentment. His lopsided smile became more pronounced.

He said nothing else; He simply let the vague knowledge of an impending consequence hang over me. I knew He would answer eventually, and when He did, there would be a price to pay. My fear grew as He went about our normal routine, removing my cuffs and holding me while He gave me food and water.

By the time He brought the melon to my lips, I was so tense that I flinched away from his hand. He handled me so tenderly, but the sadistic glint in his eyes let me know that He had something unpleasant planned for me.

"Not hungry?" He asked, removing the food before I could answer. Apprehension had risen up in my throat, blocking my vocal cords.

All that escaped my lips was a small squeak of surprise when He gripped my hips and flipped me over. He sat on the edge of the bed, and suddenly I was staring at the concrete floor, my waist bent over his knees. I squirmed in his lap, struggling to right myself. His large hand gripped my hip and his forearm pressed down on the length of my spine, firmly holding me in place.

I stopped fighting. I knew I was about to pay the price; I was about to get the answer I so desperately needed.

"I need to control you because it makes me feel alive."

He uttered the profound words as though it was a simple statement. My heart swelled, and my joy bled through my fear.

Everything I had suspected about Him was true. He didn't feel human emotions. Or at least, He hadn't. I had changed that. I was of vital importance to Him.

He was the only real thing in my world, but He couldn't be alive without me.

"I'm going to hurt you now, pet," He told me in that same even tone. "I *need* to hurt you."

Again, I understood so much more than what his words directly expressed.

He's broken. He can't feel anything without controlling me, and now He knows that I know that. I have too much power now. He needs to hurt me to feel like He's still in complete control.

His hand came down on my ass with a resounding *smack.*

"Quiet," he reprimanded.

"I-I didn't say anything, Master," I protested, the fresh tears in my eyes matching the burn of his hand on my bottom.

"I could hear you thinking." The words were disapproving, but his tone was one of fondness. "You don't have to think when you're with me. Pets don't think for themselves." His hand came down on me again, and I cried out. "Take what your Master gives you, and don't question Him." His voice turned low and feverish on the last.

I craned my neck to look up at Him. His pupils were dilated with lust, his lips parted with desire. His stunning features were illuminated by the rush of pleasure elicited by his hand upon me.

His fingers tangled in my hair, fisting it and tugging my head back.

"Eyes forward," he commanded.

I had asked my question, and He had answered. I owed Him this pain because of the terms of our agreement. But there was more than that: I *wanted* to give Him my pain. I wanted Him to know that it was okay to need me.

I needed him to realize that He cared. Then He would let me go.

"Take what your Master gives you and don't question Him."

It wasn't as difficult as it should have been to relax across his knees, submitting my body for his punishment, for his release.

He began to exact the cost I owed Him from my flesh, his hand coming down on me again and again. At first, He dispersed the blows carefully, enflaming every inch of my bottom and thighs. Then the hits began to overlap, driving the sting deeper, turning it to a relentless throb below the surface of my skin.

The pain hit a pinnacle, a place where I didn't think I could take any more. I begged Him to stop. But He didn't. He showed me that He had all the power, and there was nothing I could do to stop Him.

Realizing the utter insignificance of my words, my wants, I sank into acceptance. I stopped fighting the pain. I allowed it to flow through me, to claim all of me. My body and mind were beholden to the pain, beholden to Him.

"That's it, pet." He pressed his hand into my flesh, holding the heat there. "Accept it."

His palpable pleasure morphed the pain into something… different. Every blow hurt, but the stinging barbs turned to little tingles that raced up my spine to flood my mind.

I gasped as the high hit me. It was almost more intoxicating than the pleasure that had rushed through me when I was impaled on his cock. I was connected to Him, but this was a different kind of intimacy, one found through pain and acceptance, through control and submission. He had dominated my body when He took me, but I had met his thrusts eagerly, joining with Him in achieving our mutual pleasure. This was a complete power exchange, and I gave Him everything as I gloried in the rush of total release.

I didn't have to worry about my sanity or resisting lust or escaping Him. I didn't have to worry about anything. It wasn't trust so much as it was a complete acceptance of his control.

My consciousness retreated, leaving me floating in his power. I reveled in it.

I barely registered when the bliss-inducing blows stopped. The heat of his hand retreated, but the heat of his punishment remained simmering deep within me.

His low, lustful growl tugged me back to reality, to Him. He was my reality. My eyes fluttered open, and I drank Him in.

He flipped me onto my back, and my legs dangled over the edge of the mattress. His clothes were gone, and I could cherish every inch of him for the first time. The defined muscles I had once feared were now the most breathtaking thing I had ever seen. In that moment, I couldn't recall having seen anything at all before He came and released me from my darkness.

Every line of his body was sculpted, as sharply defined as his cheekbones. The planes of his chest gave way to rippling abs. The V of his hips was an arrow leading to the cock that had given me so much pleasure. My mouth watered at the sight of it.

His jaw appeared even stronger than usual as He bared his teeth in a possessive snarl.

I would sacrifice myself to this God a thousand times over and never regret it. The savage intensity of the inferno in his eyes was an acceptance of my offering.

He grasped my ankles and pulled my body against his. My wetness already coated my thighs, and He entered me in one thrust. My back arched on a shocked cry at the sudden impalement. His heat branded me, marking me as his own.

My legs rested against his shoulders, and He leaned forward to grip my hips. My hands closed around his, ensuring that He kept me in his hold. His fingers curled around me, but his harsh hold was somehow sweet.

He cares.

I wept with joy as He moved within me, pinning my body in place for his use. When his head dropped back with the beginnings of his own orgasm, He pinched my clit. The shock of pain made me clench around Him. He shouted out his release as my own rolled through me.

He collapsed atop me. My legs fell to either side of Him, and He remained seated deep within me, both of our bodies trembling with the little resounding jolts of our pleasure. The weight of Him upon me and the ache of bruises where my bottom pressed into the mattress enfolded me. He was all around me, and I breathed in his earthy scent with rapture.

His nose traced the line of my jaw, as though He was reveling in me as well. Then, for the first time, his lips brushed against me. The soft kiss was feather-light against my neck, but the answering ecstasy hit me with the force of a truck.

He cares.

His Journal

May 21, 1978

> *She asked me why I need to control
> her. I told her the truth. She makes
> me feel alive.*
>
> *I don't know if I can allow us to
> carry on this way any longer. I'm
> addicted to the pleasure she gives
> me. She has that power over me, and
> she knows it. I gave her pain to
> reclaim my control, but is it really
> control when she wants it, too?*
>
> *And damn it if the sight of her
> ecstasy under my harsh discipline
> didn't make me harder for her than
> ever before. I had thought I wanted
> her screams, her tears. I've gotten
> them, but not in the way I had
> expected. She screams in pleasure
> and weeps in joy.*
>
> *And that makes me… happy.*
>
> *I don't know what to do with what
> she makes me feel. Everything is so
> new, so visceral. Emotions were a*

glorious discovery at first, but now I'm enjoying them at the cost of my control. If I don't have control, the darkness will return. I can't allow that to happen. If it does, I might as well kill her and be done with it.

It might be time to break her.

Chapter 8

Kathleen

Can I escape?

He *spanked* me. Like a disobedient child. He spanked me, and I liked it.

My old disgust rolled through me in my darkness. It was a struggle to hold on to it. When I thought of the heady release I achieved from the pain of his hand striking my bottom, I flushed with remembered pleasure. It warred with the disgust the memory elicited. It almost swallowed the disgust whole.

I recognized that I was going insane.

"You're the strongest woman I've ever met." A man who had loved me once said that. That was a long time ago, in another lifetime.

My hollow laugh echoed in the darkness. I wasn't strong. I hadn't fought. Not really. I had just laid here and accepted abuse.

I had fought the crushing power of abuse before I was taken. I had overcome it with my mind; my body hadn't been strong enough to fight off my father's brute strength. What could a child do against a grown man?

I had thought that my mind would see me through this new torment. I fell back into old practices, relying on my wits to see me through.

But my captor was too intelligent. Possibly more intelligent than me. That thought rankled, but it was true. I had studied hard to gather my knowledge, but He seemed to wield an innate genius for manipulation.

My father had been stupid, uneducated. My mind had been capable of seeing me through his torment.

But Him… My mind was pathetic in comparison to His. He was always so far ahead that my efforts to resist Him were turned against me. He did it so easily, I might as well have been a child.

But I wasn't a child. Not anymore. I may not have been strong enough to fight my father, but I was a woman now. The strength of my captor's muscles had intimidated me from the very beginning, stifling thoughts of physical resistance.

Now, it seemed the only course of action available to me. He might anticipate my questions, my emotional responses, but He wouldn't be prepared for me to actually fight Him.

The element of surprise. It was all I had left.

Can I escape? It was a silent question, one I would never ask aloud. I wasn't about to ask for his permission. I knew what his answer would be. His *No, pet* would come out with an amused lilt.

I was exhausted from the efforts of formulating thoughts, especially ones of resistance.

The darkness crept in, blanketing my mind to silence once again.

When He finally came to me, I struggled to recall my plan. The rush of pleasure elicited by his first touch upon my cheek was enough to draw forth the echo of my disgust. I clung to it, desperate to remember my plan.

He noticed the change in my demeanor.

"Did my pet want to ask her Master a question?" His tone was perversely hopeful.

I shook my head. "No, Master."

Abruptly, He ripped the blindfold from my eyes. His face was twisted into a scowl, and I shrank back into the mattress.

"What have I told you about lying to me?" He demanded angrily.

"I…" I gasped. "I'm not lying, Master. I don't want to ask a question."

His scowl faded to a frown as He considered me. He cocked his head, a furrow forming in his perfectly smooth brow.

"No, you're not lying," He allowed after a long minute. "I won't force you to ask now. You'll say it when you're ready."

I'll never say it. Not to You. I won't ask if You'll allow me to escape.

"Thank you, Master," I said instead.

The lines of his face were taut with his puzzlement when He pulled the blindfold back over my eyes. Despite his evident frustration, He was as tender as ever when He uncuffed me and fed me.

Not now. Not yet.

It was too soon. I couldn't hope to fight Him while He held me in his arms. He wouldn't fully release my body until He placed me in the shower.

As He carried me to the bathroom, I began to tremble. His arms tightened around me, and his low growl gave voice to his irritation with my reticence. It must be driving Him crazy that I was keeping something from Him. He wasn't in control.

I'm driving Him *crazy?* It took effort to hold in my mad giggle. If only that were true.

My feet hit the smooth porcelain of the shower.

Now!

I wrenched off the blindfold before He could stop me. I needed my sight.

His eyes had half a second to widen in shock, and I took advantage of his moment of inaction. I knew a man's weakest point.

I brought my knee up sharply, cringing as it drove into his groin. He gasped, clutching himself as He doubled over.

I skirted around Him, forcing my disused leg muscles to steady beneath me. I almost made it to the bottom of the stairs when his furious roar echoed through the small bathroom. His feet pounded behind me.

Get to the stairs! Get to the stairs!

I was so close. So close-

My scalp screamed when his fingers closed in my hair, jerking me away from freedom.

"No!" I managed to cry out my anguish just before my back hit the wall. My skull cracked against the concrete blocks. My vision went black for the space of a second, and when sight returned, I was sprawled on the floor. His rage slammed down on me from where He towered over me.

Memory kicked in.

Don't hurt me, Daddy. Please don't hurt me. I'm sorry. I'm sorry.

My body curled into a ball, just as it had done when I was a child. My knees pressed against my chest, and my hands braced over my head, straining to protect my most vulnerable areas from his punishing blows.

I flinched and whimpered at the first contact. It took me a heartbeat to process that his hands were gently encircling my wrists, slowly prying my hands away from my face. I squeezed my eyes shut, terrified to witness the sight of his fist coming at me with enough force to crunch my bones.

"Open your eyes, pet." I was shocked at the strain in his voice.

My ingrained obedience overrode my fear. When I looked up into his eyes, the depth of pain I found in them bled into me, seeping through my own eyes to sink into my soul.

"I would never hurt you." His lips pursed as He recognized his lie. "I would never beat you. Not like that. Not like he-" He stopped abruptly. The shake of his head was sharp with anger, but I sensed it wasn't directed at me.

His red-gold glare found me again, but through the fury I saw a deep sense of betrayal. It was written in the lines around his eyes and the sad twist of his lips. Suddenly, He appeared younger, more vulnerable, than He ever had. But somehow He also appeared years older, more careworn.

"I'm sorry, Master," I heard myself whisper. Without a thought, I reached for Him. My fingers gently wiped away the tautness around his mouth, easing his pained expression.

"I don't want you to be scared of me, pet. At least, not in that way." His whispered words stunned me.

He cares.

The warmth that the thought elicited was heat, a consuming inferno. It burned through my lingering disgust, my last vestiges of resistance.

I recognized our shared pain, and the betrayal in his eyes cut at me like a knife in my heart.

He knows. He understands. Someone hurt Him, too.

How could I bring Him more pain than He had already known?

"I'm sorry, Master," I repeated.

He brushed my sweat-dampened hair back from my forehead. "Don't do that again. I might lose control, and I couldn't bear it if-" He cut himself off again, his expression going blank.

I understood that He was wrestling with his depth of emotion for me.

He cares.

"Never," I agreed fervently. "I'll stay with you, Master."

He needed me. How could I possibly leave Him when He needed me?

His Journal

May 22, 1978

>*She tried to escape me. She tried to leave me. My anger with her betrayal almost made me lose control. Yes, beating my father to death granted me that heady sense of power for the first time, but my control over her is better, more fulfilling. I'm not crushing the life out of her; I'm crushing her resistance. I'm carefully hammering her mind into the shape I wish, like a blacksmith beats upon heated, pliant metal to shape it into the implement he desires.*

>*I desire her obedience, her submission, her devotion. I don't desire to inflict fear so intense that she will be driven to madness. I don't want her to be broken.*

>*A part of me is proud of her for her rash bid for freedom. She still manages to surprise me. And the light of true submission in her eyes when she touched my face was... pleasant.*

Yes, I was right not to beat her. This complete devotion is so much better. I can hurt her, can harvest pleasure from her, for so much longer if I don't destroy her.

Chapter 9

Kathleen

Who hurt you, Master?

I had wondered what made my dark angel fall. Now I wondered *who* made Him fall.

He said He needed to control me to feel alive. Who had hurt Him so badly that He couldn't allow himself to feel anything? How deep must the scars go to cause that kind of damage to his soul?

These were the only thoughts that filtered through my perpetual night. I had given up on memories of my other life. They were painful. Or at least, they had been. Now, I only felt a strange detachment when one skittered across my mind. That life hadn't held any true pleasure as this one did. No one had ever shown me the ecstasy that He did. No one had understood my pain like He did.

When I was with Him, I didn't have to fight to make something of myself, to deny myself the most basic need for intimacy. All I had to do was submit, and Master gave me everything I needed.

When He came for me, I smiled into the darkness. He removed my blindfold, and I found Him smiling down at me in response to my own joy.

There was no more than a touch of cruelty to the twist of his lips now. I needed to know who had instilled that cruelty. Then He could finally purge it from himself. He wouldn't need to hurt me to feel alive.

He won't need me.

The thought was a knife to my gut.

No. This was for the best. He would be healed, and He would release me from my bonds. If He freed me, that didn't mean I had to leave Him. He would still need me to keep his demons at bay. He cared about me.

And I cared about Him. I wanted to fix Him.

"Who hurt you, Master?"

His smile disappeared, his lips thinning. I hadn't realized how open his eyes had become until they shuttered closed, the gleaming gold muting to dull brass. His fists curled at his sides.

I'm sorry, Master. I don't want to upset you, Master. I didn't dare speak the words aloud. Not because I feared his retribution, but because I didn't want to cause Him to retreat further into himself.

He stared down at me, and I held my breath, waiting. He looked as though He wanted to hurt me. Deeply.

Steeling my resolve, I willed the anxiety rising within me to subside. This question was too important for me to allow fear to ruin it. I wasn't sure what more Master could take from me, but He couldn't take anything if He didn't answer. That would violate the rules of his game.

The taut lines around his mouth told me that He realized the same thing. His hand twitched toward me. I wasn't sure if He wanted to strike me or if He wanted to shove me down and fuck me. Gauging by the confusion in his eyes, He wasn't sure either.

After a moment, his expression hardened. When He reached for me, it was a controlled, deliberate movement. Saying nothing, He pulled the blindfold back over my eyes.

I panicked at the loss of the sight of Him.

"Master?" His name was colored with alarm.

He moved away from me. The stairs creaked with his retreat.

"Master, wait! I'm sorry! I'm sorry!"

He ignored my cries. I screamed his name over and over, until my throat was raw, but He didn't return to me.

My anguished tears were shed for Him, not myself.

■■■

The door opened for the first time in what seemed an eternity. My stomach ached for food more acutely than it had since He first abducted me.

"Master, I-"

"Don't speak to me, slave." He cut across my croaked apology.

Slave. He had never called me that before. I was his pet. He took care of me. He cared about me.

I pressed my lips together. If I was good, He would forgive me. He had to forgive me.

He cares. He cares.

He tugged the blindfold from my eyes with none of his usual finesse. When He unlocked my cuffs, there were no tender, lingering touches upon my skin. Instead, He drew back from me immediately.

He shoved a plate of fruit across the mattress so that it rested by my face. I didn't understand why He had removed my blindfold to feed me. I didn't understand why He wasn't holding me as He usually did.

Pushing back my confusion, I opened my mouth, waiting for Him.

"Eat," He ordered shortly.

"Master-"

"What did I tell you about speaking to me, slave?"

I reached for the sliced apple with shaking hands. It had been so long since I had moved without his direction. I barely remembered how to eat without his help.

My fingers paused before bringing the fruit to my lips, and I stared at Him imploringly.

"If my slave can't follow orders, then she won't eat at all." The words were dispassionate, his voice flat.

I shoved the apple in my mouth so fast I nearly choked on it. He watched me as I ate, but his eyes were dull, his face utterly expressionless. It was as though I wasn't even a living thing.

I'm your pet, Master. You care about me. Remember? I'm sorry. I'm so sorry.

My tears flowed, but the words didn't. I would be obedient. I would be good.

"Good behavior is rewarded."

If I was good, He would reward me with his warmth again. He had to. I had known ecstasy as his pet; I would know nothing but madness as his slave.

My heart felt brittle in my chest, as though one cruel word from Him would shatter it.

When I finished the apple, He thrust a glass of water at me. I stared at it stupidly. What was I supposed to do?

"Drink it." The order was clipped, impatient.

I grasped the glass before He could remove it. My fingers brushed against his, and I allowed them to linger. I gazed up into his eyes, willing Him to feel the connection between us.

His nostrils flared, and He jerked the water away. It sloshed over the sides of the glass, spilling onto my arm.

Without a word, He set the glass down on the floor. A small cry of distress worked its way up my throat when He secured my cuffs to the headboard again. When He pulled back from me, He retrieved the water. Staring me straight in the eye, He raised it to his lips and drained the entire glass in a matter of seconds.

Tears slipped from the corners of my eyes. He was hurting so badly. I recognized his pain in his need to torture me.

"I'm sorry, Master," I whispered.

He snarled and threw the glass down. It shattered on the concrete, filling the room with the sound of his own brokenness.

"Don't speak to me, slave!"

He pulled the blindfold over my eyes. He left me again, leaving me wanting for water, for his touch, for his approval.

In the dark, my mind retreated to a place of wordless distress. All I could do was wait for Him to come back to me.

■■

I lost track of the number of times my new, cold Master came to me. His visits were perfunctory, as though His only concern was to give me the sustenance I needed to keep my heart beating. He never touched me. He watched me as I fed and washed myself.

I ached for the feel of His hands upon me. Just the sight of Him got me wet. I wasn't sure if my body hoped that my arousal would stir Him, or if it was now a Pavlovian response to His presence.

I didn't dare touch myself in front of Him, but in the dark, the desire overwhelmed me. My hands twitched in my cuffs, seeking freedom to relieve the painful throbbing of my core. My body was desperate for any sort of human contact.

I was beginning to forget what His touch felt like. The realization elicited enough panic to jolt my brain back to coherence.

There had to be some way to bring my old Master back. The man who cherished me, who touched me so tenderly, who gave me such merciful pain.

He's hurting. Someone hurt him.

A memory stirred, blurry and distant. It was more a concept than a concrete scene from my past.

Someone hurt me.

If I shared my pain with Master, maybe He would share His pain with me.

∎∎

My breathing turned fast and shallow as I listened to His approach. I didn't dare speak out of turn, but I had to fix things between us; I had to fix *Him*.

Thankfully, He spoke first. As always, He read my body easily.

"What are you thinking, slave?" My heart leapt at the note of curiosity in His voice.

"My father hurt me," I said quickly. The words were rusty issuing from my disused mouth, but they were discernable. "He beat my mother and my sister and me."

"Is this your way of telling me I'm just like your father?" He snarled, and His rage pulsed over me.

He ripped the blindfold from my eyes. I blinked to find His face looming just above me, His nose inches from mine. His red gaze burned into me with the force of His fury.

"That I'm just like *my* father?" He demanded.

"Your father hurt you, too." It was a statement, not a question.

His hand wrapped around my throat. His fingers were iron bands, but they barely pressed into my skin. His violence was restrained by a thread.

"He beat my mother to death." He spat the words at me. "I was two years old, but I remember. I remember her ruined face, her blood pooling on the floor to trickle under the door to the closet, where I hid. It wet my cheek where I stared through the crack between the door and the floorboards. I couldn't look away. I couldn't…"

He trailed off, tearing His eyes from me, as though looking away from me would allow Him to rip His inner gaze from the horrors of His past.

"You're not like him." I didn't even realize that the words were a lie. "You don't hurt me. Not really."

You need me. You care.

Suddenly, He twisted my nipple hard. I cried out at the exquisite pain of the contact.

He touched me.

My entire body, my whole heart, thrilled at His touch.

This was real. He was real. *I* was real. For a while, I had forgotten that I was capable of feeling sensation. I had begun to forget that I was alive.

He squeezed my throat incrementally. "But I need to hurt you, pet. I want you to hurt."

Pet. Not slave. I became wet in anticipation of His pain. I would accept what He gave me, would take the hurt from Him into myself.

"You're the strongest woman I've ever met."

Someone had said that to me, once. I *was* strong. Strong enough to heal Him.

Some part of me should have realized that the strength I used to value so highly had been twisted, turned in on itself. But even those soft whispers in the depths of my mind had ceased. My old lifetime was over. It might not have ever been real.

Had I existed before Master showed me true pleasure?

If He needed me to feel pain so that He could feel anything at all, then I would take it.

"Then hurt me, Master."

His groan was full of aching need. Hastily, He freed himself from his pants and settled His body over mine.

I moaned and rocked my hips up into Him in wanton invitation.

He drove inside my wet and ready sex in one rough thrust. He hadn't paused to put on a condom, and I reveled in the feel of His naked flesh inside mine. This was how it was meant to be: nothing between us. Not between our bodies and not between our souls. My soul was bound to His, enveloped by His.

His pain was my pain, and I gloried in the exchange.

He withdrew from me fully, and suddenly He was at my dark entrance. No one had ever touched this area, not even Him. I squirmed beneath Him, fear pricking at my spine despite my willingness to give Him everything.

He placed my legs against His shoulders and gripped one of my thighs hard, bracing himself on the mattress with His free hand. He held me in place and ruthlessly pressed against me.

"Let your Master in." The lustful snarl was colored with the pain of His need to enter me, to own every part of me.

With His order, familiar submission rolled through me, and I relaxed completely, ceding everything to Him.

Slowly, my body gave way as He began to penetrate me. It burned, but I remained relaxed, determined to accommodate Him. My whine of pain made His eyes flare with satisfaction, and I relaxed further. I had pleased Him.

There was a small popping sensation when His head breached me, and the burning eased. My own slickness around Him aided his progress. He rocked in and out, gaining ground with each thrust.

When He was seated fully within me, He slowly dragged out, leaving only the head of His penis inside me. My strangled moan echoed His. The sensation was strange and delicious. The sparks that awoke within that secret part of me held a bite of pain. It only served to increase my pleasure. The knowledge that He was giving me His pain made my eyes mist over with relief.

By the time He began pumping in and out in earnest, I was weeping. The rush of sensation, of the emotional connection that entwined us, was almost too much for me to bear.

But I would take it. For Him, I would shatter a thousand times and piece myself back together so that He could shatter me again.

And I did shatter. The dichotomy of pleasure and pain, the pure bliss of having His touch granted to me once again, sent me over the edge. My muscles contracted around Him as I screamed.

"Master!"

I didn't know if it was the sound of His name upon my lips or the sensation of moving inside my tight heat that brought about His own orgasm, but He followed me moments later.

He remained within me as we both shuddered and gasped. My legs wrapped around His waist, holding Him to me even as His arms wrapped around my shoulders. I longed to clutch Him to me, but my arms were still restrained.

But it was enough. It was more than enough.

His lips touched my forehead in a doting kiss.

"My sweet pet," He murmured into my hair.

I nuzzled into Him, pressing my cheek to His. Salt and earth and sex surrounded me. My legs tightened around Him.

My breathing remained ragged, but when His had slowed to a normal rhythm, He unlocked my restraints. I relished the feel of His hard chest against me as He carried me to the bathroom. He turned on the shower, testing the spray to make sure it was comfortably warm before placing me beneath it.

My knees almost buckled when He released me to remove His clothes; I hadn't stood on my own in so long. He steadied me with His strong hands around my hips, waiting until I found my feet. When He was satisfied that I wasn't going to fall, He quickly undressed, revealing His glorious body to me.

A sort of warm languor had settled in my bones, but my pulse still quickened at the sight of

Him. It seemed as though a lifetime had passed since He had last allowed me to look upon Him. In a way, it had. Another lifetime had faded completely from my consciousness in the course of my cold solitude.

He was my entire existence now.

He joined me in the shower, molding His front to my back. Soapy hands roved over my flesh, gently cleaning me after our harsh coupling. Then He did something He never had before: He handed the soap to me.

"Touch me." The order was soft, almost slurred. I turned to find that His eyes were hooded, as though He was intoxicated by the intensity of our passion.

I eagerly obeyed, my soap-slicked fingers touching every inch of Him, exploring Him more thoroughly than ever before. My hands shook with the effort after their long period of disuse, but my desire to connect with Him gave me the strength I needed to wash Him.

He was semi-erect again by the time I reached His manhood. I cleaned Him carefully, gingerly. He hissed in a breath and grabbed my wrist, pulling me away.

"Not now, pet."

He turned from me. For a moment, I thought it was in disapproval, but then He looked over His shoulder, a cool brow raised.

"Continue."

I touched His upper back, and I gasped softly. My fingers traced over thin purple lines that crisscrossed His shoulders.

His father.

I understood the sign of abuse.

I'm so sorry, Master.

But I wasn't entirely sorry. If His father hadn't broken Him, then He never would have taken me. He wouldn't need me.

The cascading water sloughed the soap off His skin, fully revealing the damage. Without thinking, I leaned forward and lightly pressed my lips to one of the marks. He tensed for a moment, a low growl rumbling through His chest to vibrate against my mouth. Before He could tell me to stop, I traced the line of it with my tongue. He relaxed against me with a sigh.

I gave each one the same loving attention, as though I could soothe the pain He had suffered when the blows were inflicted upon Him.

I was almost finished when He turned sharply. His hand closed around the back of my head and His arm wrapped around my waist, pulling me up into Him.

His mouth descended on mine with a ferocity that made our teeth click together. The kiss was unrefined, driven by hunger and deepest need. His lips grabbed at mine, His tongue seeking entrance to my mouth.

He's never done this before, I realized.

I touched my fingertips to the side of his face, calming Him. Then, I carefully caressed His lips with mine. He quickly picked up my rhythm, and soon His tongue played along the seam of my lips once again. I opened for Him, sliding my tongue along His in silent instruction.

The kiss turned hotter, fiercer as He took control. I ran my hands through His hair, tugging Him closer. His fist grasped my locks, tilting my head back so that my lips were where He wanted them.

My back was against the wall, the cool tiles kissing me with a delicious chill. It contrasted beautifully with His heat.

He gripped my bottom in both hands, lifting me, and my legs wrapped around Him to keep from falling. My arms twined around the back of His neck for support. He thrust into me abruptly, His cock claiming my core as His tongue claimed my mouth. I was impaled at both ends, completely captured by Him.

He fucked me into sweet oblivion. I shattered again.

His Journal

June 1, 1978

> *She's perfect. It was stupid of me to stop fucking her when she asked about my father. I think I was almost as crazy from the sexual denial as she was.*

> *But I'm already crazy. I was insane before I took her. I've read enough to know that.*

> *Anti-social behavior. Cruelty. Psychopath.*

> *It didn't bother me then, and it still doesn't. I'm not flawed. I'm better, stronger, smarter than other people.*

> *If anything, her new insanity makes me feel saner than I ever have. I feel things now, but I am no less cruel. She fulfills my needs in a way that makes them feel normal, natural. I am completely myself with her in a way I have never been, not even when I was alone.*

And even in her insanity, she isn't broken. Somehow, she's still her. *She is utterly obedient, but she's also affectionate, devoted. The determination that once facilitated her resistance now manifests in her determination to please me. She takes whatever I give her because she wants to make me happy. She still has her backbone, but I've twisted it against her somehow. It now serves me, not her.*

She is taking to pain beautifully, but I want to give her more. I want to see how far I can push her.

I hope she still has enough of her mind left to ask a question. I could beat her out of turn if I wished and she would take it. She would take it and thank me. But I would rather she condemn herself.

I want her to choose to take my pain.

Chapter 10

Kathleen

Do you care about me at all, Master?

My existence separated into two states: *Him* and *Not Him*.

No. That was wrong. When He wasn't with me, I didn't exist. My lungs simply continued to breathe, my heart continued to beat in the darkness. But that wasn't real. It was just a state of being.

His touch, His pleasure, His pain. They were my reality.

He fed me and washed me and fucked me. The only changes from our interactions before His long period of cold detachment were His kisses and the little pill He gave me sometimes: birth control. He no longer wore a condom, and I loved the closeness we shared when He was inside me, nothing separating us.

It was a laughable understatement to say that I was utterly enthralled. I lived to serve Him. The only point of my existence was to please Him, to help Him manage His deeply-held pain.

I was perfectly content while in His arms. Almost.

He was my everything, but there was one niggling discomfort that lurked at the back of my mind.

Does He care?

I had worked for so long to make Him care. His gentle touches, the trust He showed me by sharing His pain, His passionate kisses – they gave me hope that He did treasure me as much as I imagined.

I flashed back into existence when His fingers worked their way through my hair, finding the bottom of the blindfold and sliding it up over my brow.

His smile was one of anticipation.

"What do you want to know, pet?"

He knew. He always knew. He understood me better than I understood myself.

"Do you…" I hesitated, my cheeks heating for the first time in longer than I could recall. Embarrassment and self-consciousness were a distant memory; He owned me, and I would never be ashamed of anything that was His.

But now the sensation of uncomfortable warmth in my gut and just under my skin teased at me once again.

"Do you care about me at all, Master?" The question was small and almost frightened. I was scared of the answer. I swallowed hard, but I held his gaze, waiting through my anxiety.

He cupped my cheek in His hand, tracing the line of my cheekbone with His thumb.

"My little pet is still so brave." The pleasure and approval in His voice sent relief ripping through me on a ragged sob.

It wasn't an answer, but the sadistic red gleam of His eyes let me know that one was coming. I wasn't afraid of paying the price for my question. Fear was useless, exhausting. He would do whatever He desired regardless of my fear.

I submitted, settling down into acceptance as He unlocked my cuffs and guided me to my feet. His hands were tender upon me, but firm in supporting me. Taking my hands in His, He led me across the room, watching me almost tentatively, as a lover would before introducing His partner to something new.

"Stay." He pressed His lips to my forehead briefly and dropped my arms. I hated the loss of contact, but I obediently remained where He had placed me: an indistinct spot near one corner of my small room.

I heard Him rummaging behind me, in the direction of the bathroom. There was a cabinet beneath the sink. I had never seen Him open it, but I knew it was there. Despite my constant blindness, every inch of my room was burned into my mind, images of what He had done to me there imprinted into my psyche.

When He appeared before me again, He held a shiny length of chain. The links were thicker than those that attached my wrists to my headboard.

"I've so been hoping you had another question in you, pet," He told me with a small, secret smile.

He folded the chain in two and then tossed one end into the air. It clattered against the low wooden beam that ran across the ceiling, hooking through the open air above it to arc down on the other side. He caught it deftly before slipping the opposite ends through the loop He had created when He folded it.

By the time He turned his attention back to me, the chain was securely hooked over the beam. I met His proud grin with a quizzical stare.

He just shook His head at me slightly, as though at a particularly slow child who had yet to get the joke.

"Lift up your arms."

Still not understanding, I did as He commanded. He gripped the circular links on each of my cuffs and linked a large padlock between them, slipping it through the chain links as well. He stepped away, leaving me stretched taut before Him.

He ran a hand down the length of my side almost reverently, His rough callouses skimming from the side of my breast, down my waist, over my hip. When His touch met my upper thigh, He reached around to grab my ass, kneading my flesh between His strong fingers. I gasped and arched into Him. Wetness gathered between my legs.

I was ever at His mercy, but this new position made me particularly vulnerable. I was restrained as I usually was on my bed, but He had access to my front and back now. The hardness of His cock pressing into my belly let me know that He was enjoying the new arrangement as well.

Keeping my body flush against His with His hold on my bottom, He reached behind Him to retrieve something from His back pocket.

A whip.

He gazed deeply into my eyes, relishing the budding terror He found there.

Releasing me, He stepped back to uncoil the whip.

Crack!

It flew through the air faster than my eye could follow, and a small, frightened cry popped from my mouth at the shock of sound.

I trembled as He circled behind me. Fear flashed through my system more viscerally than it had in a long time. I submitted completely to Master, but I was afraid of the pain that I knew was coming.

"Shhh." His heat was at my back, and His arms wrapped around me. He tweaked my nipple, and it pebbled instantly under his touch. His other hand found my clit, stroking it and giving me a reassuring wash of pleasure. I leaned against Him, my head dropping back on His shoulder. His lips brushed across my exposed nape, teasing and nibbling at the sensitive spot where my neck met my shoulder.

"Yes, pet," he whispered at my ear. "I care."

The words seeped into me, through my skin and into my mind. My tears were drawn from a well at the core of my being, shedding little drops of my soul in offering to Him, giving Him everything.

The first lash hit my shoulders with a force that took my breath away. The air left my chest in a rush, and my lungs instantly collapsed. My mouth opened to unleash a scream, but I couldn't draw breath. The line of pure fire on my back sent a searing wave racing across my skin, through my entire body. Everything was pain.

The second hit landed, knocking the wind out of me all over again.

When the whip found my flesh for a third time, my scream came.

A hundred beats pounded through my aching heart in the seconds that it took for Him to bring the lash down on me again.

He gave me a fifth hit, and I thought I would die. Surely my heart would explode from its erratic pounding; surely my lungs burn up from my scorching screaming.

Then His voice was at my ear, His hands upon my waist.

"It's over, pet."

I collapsed as relief ripped through me.

It's over. It's over.

His hot tongue traced just above one of the lines of fire that throbbed across my shoulders.

"You're like me now," He murmured against my burning flesh.

Joy poured over pain, coating it like sweet syrup. He cared. He didn't just want to make me *His*. He wanted to make me *Him*. I was a part of Him now, irrevocably and inextricably bound to Him.

"Yes, Master." I pressed the words through pain-clenched teeth. "I'm you."

The marks on my back still ached where they pressed into the mattress beneath me. For a while, Master had kept me on my front when He was absent. Even if He hadn't granted me that mercy, it wouldn't have mattered. I didn't exist when He wasn't there, so things like discomfort held no meaning.

When He came to me, He rubbed salve on the wounds, soothing me and petting me.

He cared.

I lived on that knowledge. It stayed with me, even in the dark. It was a warm glow floating in my nothingness, a constant comfort.

The creak of the door heralded my return to existence.

"You down here? I want my money, you fucker." The voice was a rough rumble, as though the man was speaking through a mouthful of gravel.

And he wasn't Master.

"What the fuck?!" His footsteps pounding down the stairs was a foreign sound. It was fundamentally *wrong.*

Strange, sausage-like fingers touched my arms, tugging at the cuffs around my wrists.

"Where's the key, missy?" His breath was hot and putrid on my face. It smelled like dirt and rubbing alcohol.

I tried to jerk away from him, but I was secured as thoroughly as ever.

"Don't touch me!" I managed a strangled shriek. It had been so long since I had demanded anything, so long since I had done anything but submitted.

But this vile man wasn't Master.

"Stop squirmin'. I'm tryin' to help you, stupid bitch."

His grubby hands pushed back my blindfold, and his lumpy potato face materialized just above me.

He was touching me. No one but Master should touch me. No one else should exist.

Adrenaline rocketed through me, piggybacking on my terror. I threw my body as far forward as I could manage in my restraints, and my teeth sank into his fat cheek.

He reeled back from me with a snarl, and a second later, his wasn't the only coppery blood filling my mouth.

My cheek tore against my teeth when he backhanded me. Black fireworks burst across my vision, and my ears rang.

"You like to play rough, cunt? That why you're down here?"

He fumbled at his belt. I knew what was coming; I recognized the cruelly delighted gleam in his small black eyes.

"Master!" I cried out for Him. He had to come. He had to.

Cold hit my stomach like a block of ice. Surely Master didn't send this man to me?

No. He couldn't have. He cared. He cherished me. He loved me.

"Yeah, call me 'Master.' I like that." The disgusting man removed himself from his dirty jeans with a leer. He was short and stubby, but there was no mistaking his hardness. His eagerness to violate me.

"MASTER!" I screamed at the top of my lungs.

He would come for me. He wouldn't let this man-

His feral roar was the sweetest sound I had ever heard. My molester's eyes widened, but he didn't even have time to fully turn his head to face the threat before Master was on him.

His hands closed around the man's shoulders, pulling him from me and throwing him down on the concrete. Master was atop him in an instant. His beautiful muscles rippled and flexed as His fists came down on the man's face again and again.

The crunching sounds and agonized groans should have made my stomach turn, but I thrilled at them. I was drunk on adrenaline and Master's residual bloodlust. I was a part of Him, so everything that He was bled into me. I gloried at the sight of my attacker's blood pooling on the floor.

When the man's heels finally stopped drumming against the concrete, Master pushed himself up. He was at my side, tender concern threading through the vengeful lines of His gorgeous face.

"It's okay pet," he cooed. "He's gone."

He lovingly rubbed His bloody knuckles over my cheekbone. I couldn't help flinching as

they rubbed against the bruise where the man had backhanded me.

Master's low growl was one of barely-controlled rage, and He glanced back at the unmoving body. He glared at it for a moment, then closed His eyes and took a deep breath.

"He's gone," He repeated. "Did he… *touch* you?" Master's voice was strained on the word.

"No," I assured Him softly, wanting so badly to ease the anger that twisted His gorgeous features into something fearsome to behold.

Angry. Possessive. He cares.

"I love you, Master."

He stared down at me.

A furrow formed between His brows.

He blinked.

His eyes shone gold, and He reached for me. His fingertips brushed over my lips, as though He could better understand the words that had come from them through tactile exploration.

He blinked again.

His eyes turned to lifeless brass, and He removed His hand slowly.

"I'll be right back, pet."

He didn't replace my blindfold when He walked away from me. I wanted to protest, but it wasn't my place to question my Master.

Moments later, I was alone in the light. And I was terrified. The world was around me, but He wasn't in it.

Wrong wrong wrong.

All of my muscles tensed, and my chains rattled against the headboard as my body began to shake. My teeth were practically chattering with my panic by the time He returned.

He immediately noticed my state of distress. "Breathe, pet," He ordered with a small frown of concern.

I obeyed, drawing air into my lungs in one long drag. The sudden rush of oxygen sent me flying high, and I smiled up at Him as bliss flooded over fear.

He was with me. Master was here. Everything was all right.

The mattress dipped with His familiar weight, and He bent over me, smoothing my hair back from my face.

His eyes were enigmatic. The gold and red played through one another, making His irises flash and go dull and then flash again.

He lifted something to His lips, gripping it between His teeth.

With a little jerk of His arm, He pulled the cap off the syringe and spat it out. Fear quivered through me at the sight of the needle.

"What's that, Master?" I asked the question without a thought. I no longer feared any consequence. I would pay any price He demanded of me. I longed for His consequences. They meant that He would touch me. And then He would take care of me.

His expression was almost… sad. My heart squeezed for Him.

He eased the needle into my upper arm and pressed the plunger down slowly.

"This is your last consequence," He told me softly.

What?

What did He mean by that?

"Master…" His name was thick on my tongue, but I managed to force it to slur out of my lips.

"Shhh, pet. It's okay." He reassured me as He had done so many times before, even during the time when I had hated Him. My other lifetime.

His fingers worked through my hair in a steady rhythm as blackness seeped into me. It was different from my usual blackness. Heavier. More final.

"I love you, Master."

I couldn't form the words, but I willed them to shine out through my eyes and into His. They flashed gold.

I sank into darkness.

▪▪ ▪

"Kathleen! Oh, my god! Kathleen!"

A familiar voice shrieked in my ear. Familiar hands grasped my shoulders, shaking me.

Familiar. Familiar and *wrong.*

My eyelids were heavy, but I forced them to open.

Master. I had to find Master.

I blinked hard, and the world came swirling in to existence. But it wasn't existence, because He wasn't here.

Most people would consider it to be dark, but the indigo shades of the night were far brighter than my comfortable blackness. Something cool and damp and springy was beneath my naked body.

Grass.

A woman was leaning over me, her hot tears falling on my cheeks.

Bea. My sister.

"John!" She screamed over her shoulder. "John, call an ambulance!"

The silhouette of a man filled the doorway to the house. My heart leapt.

Master.

But then the man stepped out into the night to join his wife on their front lawn, and I realized I was wrong.

Understanding coalesced slowly, starting as a sick feeling in my gut and oozing outward. When it finally hit my brain, terror and anguish slammed into me.

"MASTER!"

I fought against the drugs lingering in my system, fought to get up, to find Him. My sister held me down, whispering panicked reassurances.

"MASTER!" I wailed his name over and over, screaming it out into the world.

He'll come for me. He has to come for me. He cares. He cares...

He didn't come. He didn't care.

Chapter 11

The Mentor

June 4, 1978

I touched the flame to the tip of the cigarette, trying to catch it alight. They were my father's cigarettes. I had never smoked before, but I had heard they calmed the nerves.

My shaking hands were proof that I could use that. They also made me fail in the attempt. With a curse, I flung the unlit cigarette away. I didn't need anything that used to belong to my father, anyway. Not his cigarettes, not this house, not the farm.

I didn't want any of it. Not anymore. Not without Her.

My fist lashed out, and I punched the wall. The pain of my knuckles splitting helped to calm me.

I didn't need Her, either. She was the reason I was like this. Out of control. Confused. *Hurting.*

I punched the wall again.

She hadn't hurt *me*. I hurt Her. That was our arrangement. And now I had hurt Her in the deepest way possible: I freed Her.

She said she loved me. I had no use for Her after that. She wasn't broken, but She was ruined for me.

She ruined me.

Snarling, I grabbed up the pack of cigarettes and pulled out a new one.

No. She had ruined our game. I couldn't win if She *loved* me. I had demanded Her obedience, had been amused by Her devotion. But Her love...

I dropped the cigarette and reached out for the lock of hair that lay on the mattress before me. My fingers bushed over the silky auburn strands. I had secured it with baling twine, but that wouldn't do. It was rough against my fingers. Too rough to bind such soft beauty.

I stroked Her hair idly, for a moment imagining that She lay beneath me.

I jerked my hand away. I didn't need Her beneath me. I would find another woman, another pet.

No. Not a pet. That had been my mistake. I had tamed Her, but I hadn't broken Her. Even a tamed animal has some sense of free will. I needed a toy that I could break and reassemble and break again, until she was finally too shattered to satisfy my needs. Then there would be another.

Yes. That was what I would do. I would control them completely, and I would keep the darkness at bay. I would be able to breathe again, and I wouldn't be so goddamn *alive* that my emotions overran me.

I would learn to control them as well.

I couldn't stay on the farm. Especially not now that I had killed Dick.

My fists clenched at my sides. I wanted to murder the motherfucker all over again. If he hadn't come barging in looking for my father, She might not have told me She loved me. If my father hadn't been a piss-poor drunk who owed the moonshiner money, he never would have come.

My father. It always came back to that bastard. He was another one I would relish killing again. And again and again and again.

But the women would have to suffice. I had to be careful. I didn't intend to end up in jail. I needed a job in a big city. Maybe a job in law enforcement. I could be sure to cover my tracks more easily that way.

But most of all, I needed to forget about *Her.*

"Fuck!"

I was fondling Her hair again.

Why hadn't I just killed Her? I should have killed Her. It was stupid, risky, sending Her back to Her sister.

Killing Her would have been a mercy. I let Her go because I wanted to hurt Her.

She loved me, and now She would have to live without me. What worse pain could I inflict on Her than that?

I slipped the cigarette between my lips and flicked the lighter.

My eyes fell on the lock of hair again. It glinted red in the soft light of the tiny dancing flame.

I growled my frustration, and the cigarette fell from my lips. I touched the fire to the lustrous strands. They crackled softly, flaring orange before curling to grey ash.

There. She was gone. Eradicated from my life in every way.

I rubbed my hand over my sternum. There was the strangest ache in the center of my chest. Where my heart was supposed to be.

Epilogue

Kathleen

April 2, 2014

"Kathleen. Baby. Wake up."

My scream was still warm on my lips when I jerked to consciousness. Tears began to stream down my face.

"It's okay, baby. It was just another nightmare."

Charlie gently wiped the wetness from my cheeks, but his voice was heavy with weariness. He had been dealing with my nightmares for the last thirty-five years.

But what he didn't know was that they weren't nightmares; they were the sweetest dreams. Dreams of pain and pleasure and the ultimate peace of complete submission. I wept for the loss of the dream, for the cruel return to reality.

"Did I wake the kids?" I asked hoarsely.

"No," Charlie mumbled sleepily. "Jim's at Northwestern and Paul's in New York, remember?"

I ran a shaky hand through my hair.

"Right. Sorry, dear. You can go back to sleep. I know you have to work early."

You have to work early, and I have to sit here, wondering what to do with myself. Like I always do.

Charlie settled back down and closed his eyes, satisfied that I had been comforted and his duty had been fulfilled. His arm hooked around my waist in sleep with the easy familiarity of long companionship.

When I looked down at my husband, something like affection stirred in my chest. For thirty-five years, Charlie's hands had touched my body. Sometimes, his heart even brushed against mine. But my soul… Charlie had never come close.

My soul belongs to Master, always and forever.

The End

What is The Mentor up to now? What is His true identity? FBI agents Katherine Byrd and Reed Miller will be hunting Him down in *Master* (An *Impossible* Novel) (Coming Soon!)

Want a taste of what The Mentor has been up to? Check out *Knight* (An *Impossible* Novel)!

A woman shattered...

Abducted. He took me and broke me. I was his plaything, his possession. If I did ever have a name, I don't remember it now.

Slaves don't have names.

A savior's obsession...

My new Master stole me away from the man who tormented me. He saved me and took me for himself. His touch keeps me sane. His control keeps me grounded in reality. He demands that I piece the shards of myself back together.

But I don't want to be myself again. I want to be *his*. I've found my salvation in his obsession, my freedom in his captivity.

Will his brand of rescue leave me more broken than ever?

Excerpt

I used to think pain wasn't real. At least, not in the sense of being a tangible thing. It was just the result of my primal brain's in-built response to inform me that damage was being inflicted on my body. If I trusted the person who was giving me pain, then I knew he wasn't going to damage me. If I understood my pain, it stopped being something to fear and became something... interesting. I could master the hurt and ride the high of the adrenaline that flooded my system. I could enter subspace, that gloriously blank place where nothing existed but the sweet endorphins released by the pain that I embraced.

But then He came along and turned that all on its head. He enjoyed administering pain to torture, not to pleasure. And I couldn't trust Him not to inflict damage. He claimed He didn't like it when I forced Him to damage me; He didn't want to mar his property. But that didn't mean He wasn't willing to do so in order to get what He wanted.

I had tried to fight the pain for so long, to hold on to my conviction that it wasn't real. It couldn't hurt me if I didn't let it. But He gave me so much that it overwhelmed me, claiming all of my senses until my whole world was agony. I was perpetually trapped in some twisted, inverted form of subspace where nothing existed but the pain, but it gave me no pleasure.

My only reprieve was the sweet reward that came with the merciful sting of a needle. If I was good, if I obeyed and screamed prettily enough, then He would give me my reward. I lived for it; that was the only time I *was* alive.

But I had become so dependent on it that now the denial of my reward was just as terrible as the agony He gave me. It had been so long since I had gotten my last fix.

Tonight, Master was testing me. He wanted to see just how obedient I was. He wanted the satisfaction of seeing just how thoroughly He had broken me.

I was broken. And I didn't even care. All I cared about was my reward. Right now, my need for it was so acute that my insides were twisting and my skin was on fire. I was desperate to give Him whatever He wanted so I could get my fix. If He hadn't ordered me to stand in the corner quietly and wait for Him to return, then I would have been curled up on the floor sobbing.

But I wasn't ensconced in the stark loneliness of the pitch black dungeon that had become my home, and I didn't have the luxury of going to pieces. His order for my silence denied me even the right to voice my agony. He had brought me out in public for the first time, and I recognized the place where He had brought me as a BDSM club. He would be able to torment me here in front of dozens of strangers, and no one would stop Him.

The thought of shouting out a safe word or screaming for help didn't even cross my mind. All I could think about was when He would come back and doing my best to please Him so that He would grant me my reprieve. He had been gone for so long, and I was starting to panic.

And now a strange man was talking to me, threatening to hurt me if I didn't tell him my name. But I didn't have a name. If I did ever have a name, I didn't remember it now. I was a slave, and slaves don't have names.

Knight is now available!

Also by Julia Sykes

The *Impossible* Trilogy
Monster
Traitor
Avenger

Impossible: The Original Trilogy

Angel (A Companion Book to *Monster)*

The *Impossible* Novels
Savior
Knight
Rogue (Coming Soon!)

Dark Grove Plantation (The Complete Collection)

CPSIA information can be obtained at www.ICGtesting.com
Printed in the USA
LVOW01s1705300714

396753LV00021B/878/P